the joke's on us

MACDONALD HALL

The Macdonald Hall Series

GORDON KORMAN

the joke's on us

MACDONALD HALL

Previous title:
Something Fishy at Macdonald Hall

Cover photos by
Rodrigo Moreno and Luis Borba

Photo-illustration by
Yüksel Hassan

Scholastic Canada Ltd.
Toronto New York London Auckland Sydney
Mexico City New Delhi Hong Kong Buenos Aires

Scholastic Canada Ltd.
175 Hillmount Road, Markham, Ontario L6C 1Z7, Canada

Scholastic Inc.
555 Broadway, New York, NY 10012, USA

Scholastic Australia Pty Limited
PO Box 579, Gosford, NSW 2250, Australia

Scholastic New Zealand Limited
Private Bag 94407, Greenmount, Auckland, New Zealand

Scholastic Ltd.
Villiers House, Clarendon Avenue, Leamington Spa,
Warwickshire CV32 5PR, UK

National Library of Canada Cataloguing in Publication
Korman, Gordon
[Something fishy at Macdonald Hall]
        The joke's on us / Gordon Korman.
(MacDonald Hall series)
Previously published under title: Something fishy at Macdonald
Hall.
ISBN 0-439-96721-X
        I. Title. II. Title: Series: Something fishy at Macdonald
Hall.
III. Korman, Gordon. MacDonald Hall series.
PS8571.O78J63 2004   jC813'.54   C2004-900760-2
TO COME

6 5 4 3 2 1   Printed in Canada   04 05 06 07 08

contents

Chapter 1

over the hill

"Take my word for it, Bruno — you're not going to like him."

The speaker was Boots O'Neal. He and Bruno Walton, his longtime roommate and friend, were hanging movie posters on the walls of room 306 of Macdonald Hall.

Bruno spat out a thumbtack. "Of course I'll like him. You're just saying that because he's your brother."

"No, I'm not."

"Yes, you are," Bruno insisted. "I mean, look at me. I hate my sister, and everybody else says she's the sweetest kid on earth. It's human nature."

"You don't know Edward," Boots said flatly.

"Sure I do!"

"You've only met him twice. And he was on his best behaviour because it was vacation and my folks were around. The kid is crazy!"

"He's totally normal," Bruno countered. He took a step back to admire the new decor. "I think this one's a little crooked."

"It's fine," Boots retorted. "Dormitory 3 is crooked."

Bruno slipped into the shoe he'd been using as a hammer. He breathed deeply. "I envy your brother — young, new, first year at Macdonald Hall — he's got his whole life ahead of him."

Boots had to laugh. "And we're grandfathers, I suppose?"

"We have so much to teach him," Bruno raved on. "We can show him the ropes."

"Oh, sure," said Boots sarcastically. "He should really listen to us. We've been in trouble more than any two guys in the history of the Hall. We've washed more dishes, picked up more garbage, raked more leaves and shovelled more snow. And we definitely hold the record for being chewed out by the Fish."

"The Fish," said Bruno, smiling at the mere thought of William R. Sturgeon, the Headmaster. "Your brother hasn't even met the Fish yet! Were we ever that young?"

"Yes, we were," growled Boots. "It was a better life."

Bruno looked annoyed. "Your problem, Melvin, is that you're a crab. As soon as new student orientation is over, Edward will drop by here, the three of us will get along great and all your whining and complaining will be for nothing."

The words were barely out of his mouth when the door

flew open, and there stood Edward O'Neal. He looked very much like a younger version of Boots — blond, blue-eyed, with a sleek, athletic build.

"Eddie!" Bruno greeted the newcomer. "How's it going? Remember me? Bruno!" He bounded over and dealt Boots's brother a hearty slap on the back.

Edward's blue eyes crossed and rolled back in his head. Without a sound, he crumpled to the floor and lay there, unmoving.

Bruno stared, bug-eyed. "What did I do? What happened? I didn't hit him that hard! Call Nurse Hildegarde! Dial 911! . . . "

"Bruno — " Boots began patiently.

"We've got to keep him warm till the ambulance comes!" Bruno howled hysterically. "Quick, get a blanket!"

From the floor, Edward reached up, pulled the top sheet from Boots's bed and handed it to Bruno.

"Thanks!" gasped Bruno, covering up the victim. He froze. "Hey, wait a minute — "

Edward rose to his feet, dusting himself off.

Boots grimaced. "Come on, Edward. Why do you have to pull that weird stuff on the first day?"

Edward regarded the dumbfounded Bruno. "I'm waiting for the fun to start. The laugh-a-minute thrills. The topsy-turvy roller coaster of excitement."

Bruno found his voice at last. *"What?"*

"For half my life, every phone call, every letter home, was full of 'Bruno says,' and 'Bruno did' and how great and how cool it was to be at Macdonald Hall with Bruno," sneered Edward. "Well, here I am, on the spot with the Lord of Coolness himself. And I've got to tell you — I'm not impressed." And he turned on his heel and left.

The stunned silence that followed was broken by Boots's voice. "I told you you weren't going to like him."

* * *

Bruno and Boots crouched in the bushes outside their window, scouting the darkened campus.

"All clear," whispered Bruno.

Keeping low to the ground, they snaked along the edge of Macdonald Hall property, scampered across the road and scaled the wrought-iron fence that surrounded Miss Scrimmage's Finishing School for Young Ladies.

Bruno picked up a handful of pebbles and tossed them at a second-story window. No response.

Boots frowned. "Didn't Cathy and Diane know we'd be dropping by tonight?"

"Give it a few minutes," Bruno shrugged. "Maybe there's a teacher around, or something."

They retreated to the shadows of Miss Scrimmage's nearby apple orchard, and sat down to watch the window and wait.

"You know," said Bruno, "I've been thinking about Eddie."

Boots made a face. "Why? I don't, if I can possibly avoid it. And by the way, it's 'Edward.'"

Bruno nodded. "Yeah. He's a real jerk, and all that, but I understand him. This is his first time away from home. He's probably really scared. And he wants everybody to like him."

"Well, he made a great start today," Boots grunted. "I thought you were going to rip his lungs out."

"He's not so bad," chuckled Bruno. "He'll settle down. We'll introduce him to all the guys. Maybe we'll even bring him over here one night." He glanced at his watch. "Hey, what's keeping the girls?"

Boots stood up. "Maybe we should come back tomorrow."

"Nothing doing. The window's open. We'll wait for them inside." He began to stride toward the building.

Boots followed, listing the reasons why this was a bad idea. "Maybe their room got changed . . . maybe they haven't arrived at school yet . . . maybe Miss Scrimmage is up there with her shotgun — "

But Bruno was already shinnying up the drainpipe. Breathing a silent prayer, Boots started up after him.

Bruno swung a leg over the sill, and let himself into the room, helping Boots in behind him.

"Well, they've definitely moved in," said Boots, peering into a closet that was full of clothing. Bruno snapped his fingers. "I've got it. They knew we were coming, and they're raiding the kitchen to put up a big spread. Let's go surprise them."

"Aw, c'mon," moaned Boots. "It's one thing to sneak in here; it's another to go wandering around Scrimmage's in the middle of the night! Let's wait."

But once again, he ended up following Bruno's lead. They navigated the dim, carpeted halls, slid down the bannister of the main staircase and stepped into the ornate dining room. On tiptoe, they made their way among the round tables and paused at the door to the kitchen. There was the sound of muffled laughter and quiet singing.

"See!" said Bruno triumphantly. "I told you they were expecting us. It's a party!"

He booted open the swinging door, and prepared to bound inside. He froze.

About twenty girls were assembled, eating sandwiches, drinking pop and singing along with a lone visitor, who was strumming on a ukulele.

Bruno stared. The guest of honour was Edward O'Neal.

Wham! The big door swung back, catching him full in the face. He staggered away, giving Boots a clear view of the festivities as the door swung the other way.

"*Edward?*"

The two boys ran into the kitchen. Boots's little brother was flanked by Cathy Burton on his right and Diane Grant on his left. On the counter in front of him sat an enormous slab of triple-chocolate cake.

"Hey, dudes," Cathy greeted. "Meet Edward. He's new at the Hall."

"These are the two guys we were telling you about," Diane informed Edward.

Edward regarded them critically. "Come to think of it, I saw them over there in Dormitory 3. They were crocheting doilies."

This got a big laugh from the girls.

"Oh, shut up, Edward!" snapped Boots. "Look, girls, he's my kid brother, okay?"

At this news, Edward did another one of his phoney faints. He rolled off his chair to the floor, dropping his ukulele as he fell. This got a standing ovation from the girls.

"Edward . . . " said Boots warningly.

Bruno managed a brave smile. "Come on, Boots, back off. All the kid needs is a little patience and understanding."

Edward was on his feet again. "Why don't you two old men go home and take a nap? Face it — you're over the hill. It's time for a new generation."

It took Boots, Cathy and Diane to remove Bruno's hands from around Edward's throat.

"Let go of me, Boots!" Bruno ordered. "And prepare to become an only child!"

"Pick on someone your own size, Bruno Walton!" cried Diane in outrage.

Bruno strained forward. "Let me at him!"

Edward made a big show of yawning, then checked his watch. "Well, I guess I'd better call it a night."

"You're not going to bed until after the autopsy!" Bruno roared.

"Don't be such a bully!" snapped Cathy.

"Goodnight, all," Edward called. "Thanks for your hospitality." He took three casual steps, and then broke into a sprint across the dining room.

"Come back here!" Bruno tore free, and launched himself in pursuit of the fleeing Edward. Boots and the girls rushed after them.

Footsteps and heavy breathing echoed through the halls, but there were no shouts. No one wanted to wake up Miss Scrimmage and her staff.

Bruno and Boots had been in Miss Scrimmage's school many times and knew the layout by heart. But Edward was lost. Around and around the main floor he went, at the head of the chase. Finally, he spied a back staircase, and made a dash for it.

Diane gasped. "That's Miss Scrimmage's suite!" But everyone who heard her already knew that. And the boys were out of earshot, halfway up the stairs.

A diabolical grin appeared on Cathy's face. "This is going to be our best year yet! Who says education can't be exciting?"

The boys reached the second floor and hit the hall running. They were at top speed when a door opened, and Miss Scrimmage stepped out into their path.

Edward hit the brakes and stopped dead. Bruno slammed into Edward from behind, and Boots nearly tripped over the two of them. The three froze there, hanging onto each other for support. In his misery, Boots caught sight of Cathy and Diane crouched on the top step. Diane looked petrified; Cathy winked.

"Oh, my goodness," the Headmistress mused, adjusting her hairnet and tightening the belt on her robe. "I can't see a thing without my glasses. Now, where did I put my Cream of Wheat?" She began to feel her way around a small kitchen alcove.

Bruno drew in a shaky breath, about to sneeze. Like lightning, a finger — Edward's — appeared under his nose to stifle the impulse. Boots's sigh of relief shook all three of them.

"Ah, here it is," Miss Scrimmage announced. She started back toward her bedroom. But the spoon slipped off the tray, and landed on the carpet with a soft thud. She bent down and felt around with her free hand. Instead of the spoon, her fingers closed upon the toe of Edward's sneaker.

"A-choo!" Bruno's sneeze came out at last.

"A-a-a-augh!" shrieked Miss Scrimmage, tossing her tray in the air.

Boots grabbed Bruno with one hand and Edward with the other and headed for the stairs.

Cathy whispered, "We'll cover for you!" She and Diane ran to their Headmistress, who was screaming and picking Cream of Wheat out of her curlers.

"Oh, Miss Scrimmage! Oh, Miss Scrimmage! You were brilliant!"

The Headmistress stopped shrieking and looked up. "I – I – I was?"

Cathy nodded earnestly. "The way you threw oatmeal at those burglars and scared them away — you saved us! You're a hero!"

"It was Cream of Wheat, dear," said Miss Scrimmage, resettling herself like a hen on a nest. "And I have some information for you: those were no ordinary burglars. Those were marauders from Macdonald Hall."

"No!" Cathy and Diane pretended disbelief.

"Yes, indeed," the Headmistress confirmed. "And you may believe that Mr. Sturgeon will be hearing from me first thing in the morning!"

* * *

All the way back to Macdonald Hall, Bruno was seething. "So we're old men, eh? Over the hill? Well, tonight two old men saved your butt from Miss Scrimmage!"

Edward was outraged. "Saved *my* butt? I'm not the one who sneezed in her face!"

"But you are the idiot who blundered right into her private hallway!" Bruno accused. "If she'd had her shotgun, we'd all be part of the wall!"

"Stay away from Scrimmage's!" Boots hissed.

Edward raised big innocent eyes. "Like you do?"

"Look," said Bruno. "This is the way it is: out of respect for the O'Neal family, I've decided to let you live. But keep out of my face. And don't you ever call me 'old man' again!"

"Yes, O Aged One," deadpanned Edward, and scampered off to Dormitory 1.

Boots sighed miserably. "So sue me. You can't choose your relatives."

Chapter 2

a no-brainer

William R. Sturgeon, Headmaster of Macdonald Hall, limped down the stairs of his cottage, leaning on a wooden cane. Settling himself at the kitchen table, he peered between the ruffled curtains and harumphed at the cloudy fall morning.

"Barely Labour Day and it's already freezing."

His wife set a cup of coffee in front of him. "Good morning to you, too, William," she said brightly.

"I should have retired last year," Mr. Sturgeon went on, as though no one had spoken. "We could be in Florida now, lying on the beach. We've earned it."

Mrs. Sturgeon laughed. "You loathe the beach, William. You always get sand all over your tie."

"Very funny," grumbled her husband. "But the fact remains that there's nothing for me at Macdonald Hall anymore."

His wife looked distressed. "How can you say such a thing? This is *your school!*"

"It would run perfectly well without me," he insisted. "Everything that happens here is automatic. For example, I ran into Elmer Drimsdale yesterday and automatically congratulated him on winning the Summer Science Fair. I had no proof that he even entered!"

"But of course he did," Mrs. Sturgeon put in soothingly. "And of course he won first prize."

"That's my point exactly," said the Headmaster. "I knew that. I know everything. I know Peter Anderson struggled in summer school; I know Sidney Rampulsky broke at least one bone during vacation; I know Walton and O'Neal have already paid a visit to their friends over at Miss Scrimmage's school. There's no challenge, Mildred. My life has become, as they say, a 'no-brainer.'" He sighed. "And then there's this medical condition."

His wife cracked an egg hard enough to pulverize it. "It's an ingrown toenail, William. Your 'medical condition' is not exactly life threatening."

Mr. Sturgeon squared his shoulders stubbornly. "That's easy to say when it's on someone else's foot. It happens to be extremely painful."

"You're such a baby," she accused. "Why don't you just call up the doctor and schedule the surgery?"

Her husband set his jaw and said nothing.

"And how dare you reduce our boys to guesses and accusations?" his wife went on. "You have no proof that

Bruno and Melvin were off campus last night."

The Headmaster smiled mirthlessly. "I don't have any proof that the sun will rise tomorrow, but I expect to see it. I'm surprised we haven't heard from Miss Scrimmage to complain about the intruders."

"Now, that's just silly — "

Ding-dong.

Mrs. Sturgeon hurried to the door. "Don't get up, dear. I'll see who it is."

"I *know* who it is," he grumbled.

There were voices in the hall, and then his wife reappeared with Miss Scrimmage in tow. "Look, William. We have company."

"Miss Scrimmage — what a surprise. How may I help you?"

Miss Scrimmage removed her white gloves and feathered hat, sat down at the table and accepted a cup of coffee. "Mr. Sturgeon," she began, "alas, this is not entirely a social call."

"Ah," said Mr. Sturgeon noncommittally.

"Indeed. Last night, three of your students broke into my school and terrorized my poor defenceless girls. Fortunately, I was able to subdue them with a bowl of Cream of Wheat."

Faint indications of a smile tugged at the Headmaster's lips, but overall he remained stern. "How resourceful of you."

"And so," Miss Scrimmage went on, "I must insist that you identify the guilty parties and mete out the appropriate punishment."

Mr. Sturgeon sat forward in his chair. "An excellent

suggestion. Unfortunately, the Macdonald Hall Cream of Wheat detector is not working."

Miss Scrimmage rose in a huff. "You mock me, sir!"

"Would you care for some toast and gooseberry preserves?" put in Mrs. Sturgeon solicitously.

"Madam," said Mr. Sturgeon, "if you have an accusation, make it. But I will not start a witch hunt without proof that any of my boys were involved."

"I should have known better than to expect cooperation from you!" shrilled Miss Scrimmage. She flounced out, slamming the cottage door behind her.

"William, I'm ashamed of you," said Mrs. Sturgeon. "Why do you bait that poor lady? You know she only becomes hysterical."

"And the fact that I knew she was coming? And why? Have you nothing to say to that?"

"Well — " his wife admitted, "yes, you were right. Except you predicted it would be Bruno and Melvin, and Miss Scrimmage said there were three."

"There is another O'Neal at Macdonald Hall this year," replied the Headmaster. "This must have been a training mission for him." His eyes came to rest on Miss Scrimmage's hat and gloves, which lay forgotten on the counter. "Who dresses that woman? Somewhere there must be a barn owl running around naked!"

"You're so smug," his wife complained. "Couldn't you be wrong just once in a while?"

Her husband regarded her earnestly. "Macdonald Hall can't seem to surprise me anymore. I think that's the sign that it's time to retire."

* * *

"Way to go, Bruno and Boots!"

The two boys were waiting in the cafeteria line the next morning when Pete Anderson awarded each of them a handshake of congratulations.

"Yeah, that was great!" chimed in Rob Adams from up by the silverware bin.

"Now I know I'm back at the Hall," laughed Chris Talbot.

Boots was mystified. "What's going on?"

"Ha!" Bruno was triumphant. "We're *somebody* in this school, Boots. I only wish your moronic kid brother was here to see the kind of respect we get."

"Yeah, but what are they talking about?" Boots persisted. "They can't know about Scrimmage's the other night."

"Good one!" called Gary Potts. "Man, I laughed. I thought the harpoon was a really nice touch."

Bruno frowned. "Harpoon?"

They piled up two trays with muffins and cereal, and headed for the usual corner table. There a group of their closest friends interrupted their own breakfast to stand up and applaud the newcomers.

"I don't get it," said Boots. "What's everybody making such a big deal about?"

Mark Davies, who was editor of the school newspaper, led them to the window that faced the Faculty Building and the statue of Sir John A. Macdonald that was the centrepiece of the campus. Someone had dressed the statue in a scuba suit, complete with face mask, air tank, flippers and spear gun.

"Oh," said Bruno. "*That* harpoon."

Boots laughed. "It's a great joke, guys, but we didn't do it."

There were guffaws all around the table.

"Sure you didn't," mumbled big Wilbur Hackenschleimer from behind a triple stack of pancakes.

School genius Elmer Drimsdale was also impressed. "Certain alterations would have to have been made for the diving suit to fit on the statue," he observed. "How did you calculate where to make the cuts?"

"We didn't," shrugged Bruno, taking his seat at the head of the table. "Much as I'd like to take credit for it, this gag was pulled by somebody else."

"Hey, Boots," piped up Mark, "how does Edward like Macdonald Hall?"

"Hold it," interrupted Bruno. "This is Rule Number One: no one mentions that little creep in my presence."

"So," said Boots, anxious to change the subject, "how was everybody's summer?"

"Lousy." Pete Anderson made a face. "I was stuck in summer school to pull up my grades, and I just squeaked through by the skin of my teeth."

"I had a concussion," announced Sidney Rampulsky.

This got a big laugh. Sidney's clumsiness was legend at Macdonald Hall.

Sidney was outraged. "It's not funny, guys! A mosquito landed on my nose, and when I slapped it, I clobbered my head with the cast." He looked up as the laughter grew. "Did I mention that I broke my arm?"

"I fell in love," said Elmer solemnly.

Everybody stopped eating and stared.

"Way to go, Elm," approved Bruno. "I always knew the right amoeba would come along someday."

Elmer's eyes took on a distant look, and a goofy grin

appeared on his face. "I met her at the Summer Science Fair. There was romance in the air — or maybe it was formaldehyde from the dissected frog in the experiment beside ours. I turned to borrow litmus paper, and that's when I met Marylou Beakman. Her project came eighty-seventh, but the judges erred badly. I would have placed it no lower than seventy-first."

Boots bit back a snicker. "She's into science, too, eh? You guys must have a lot to talk about."

Elmer turned beet-red. "Talk?"

"You didn't even talk to her?" asked Sidney incredulously.

Elmer hung his head. "It wasn't my fault. I was getting ready to say something after the judging, but I was afraid she would think I was dreary and boring. I wanted to show her the real me."

"But that is the real you!" blurted Pete.

"I know," Elmer admitted sheepishly. "That's why I went to the bathroom to think of some interesting things to say. When I came back, she was gone."

"Aw, Elm," Bruno groaned. "You let her slip away. Now you're never going to see her again."

Elmer peered at him earnestly through his thick glasses. "But Marylou goes to Miss Scrimmage's Finishing School for Young Ladies. I have all year to work up the courage to talk to her."

Mark stood up and placed his tray on the kitchen conveyor belt. "I'd better get going," he told the group. "I want to get a picture of Sir John A. in the scuba suit for the school paper. I've got the perfect headline: SOMETHING FISHY AT MACDONALD HALL."

"Something's *always* fishy at Macdonald Hall," grumbled Wilbur. "Namely the guy who runs the place."

Boots snapped to attention. "The Fish! Hey, Bruno, you don't think he's going to blame it on us, do you?"

"Why would he do that?" asked Bruno absently.

"For the same reason everybody else did — it's always us!"

Bruno laughed. "You're getting paranoid, Melvin. No one's blaming us for anything."

At that moment, Larry Wilson, the office messenger, joined them at the table.

Boots looked up. "Hi. I thought you were on duty this morning."

"This is duty," Larry said grimly. "The Fish wants to see you guys in his office — right away."

* * *

Bruno and Boots sat on the hard wooden bench in the Headmaster's office, waiting for Mr. Sturgeon.

"This is so great!" Bruno chortled.

Boots stared at him. "What's so great about being called in by the Fish?"

"Don't you get it? We're *innocent!* For the first time ever, we can look the Fish in the eye and say that we didn't do it."

"Didn't do what?" came an all-too-familiar voice. The Headmaster limped into the office, leaning on a wooden cane.

Bruno jumped to his feet. "Sir! What happened? Are you all right?"

"Perfectly all right, thank you. It is a medical condition. Now, kindly regale me with the story of what you have not done."

They watched as he limped to his chair and eased into it.

"Well, sir," said Bruno, "we didn't put the scuba suit on the statue of Sir John A. I know it's our style, and you might even say it's got us written all over it. But we didn't do it."

"Honest, sir," added Boots.

The Headmaster was taken aback. Certainly, Walton and O'Neal were his most mischievous students. But they had never attempted to lie their way out of anything. Bent the truth? Yes. Side-stepped it? Always. But an out-and-out lie was not their style.

"Very well," said the Headmaster finally. "I have come to trust you boys over the years, and your word is enough for me. For example, if I were to inquire if you were involved in the incident at Miss Scrimmage's last night . . . "

"You know, sir," said Bruno carefully, "with all the excitement of a new school year, it's kind of hard to remember where you were at any given time."

"Shall I take that as a confession?" asked Mr. Sturgeon.

"Yes, sir," chorused the two boys.

Mr. Sturgeon pronounced sentence. "Three days' dishwashing, beginning with dinner tonight. You are dismissed."

Bruno and Boots fled the office and left the Faculty Building by the nearest exit. They slowed down to watch a group of groundskeepers remove the scuba gear from the statue.

"Three days' dishwashing!" said Bruno in disgust.

"What a drag," Boots agreed.

"Are you kidding?" Bruno exclaimed. "It's nothing! Last

year we would have gotten two weeks for rousting Miss Scrimmage. Plus punishment essays!"

Boots was mystified. "You want to go back in there and tell him it's not enough?"

"Don't you get it?" Bruno persisted. "He's hobbling on a cane; he lets us off easy. Something's wrong with Mr. Sturgeon, and we're going to get to the bottom of it!"

"We can't mess around in the Fish's private life," Boots protested. "He won't stand for it."

"He won't even know," Bruno assured him. "We'll start by asking Larry to keep his ears open around the office . . . "

Chapter 3

the voodoo curse

Phil, the assistant kitchen chief, exchanged high fives with Bruno and Boots as they reported for dishwashing duty.

"My buddies! How was your summer? I knew you'd be here soon, but the first day? What was the rap — the scuba suit on Sir John A.?"

"Scrimmage's," shrugged Boots.

"Yeah?" laughed Phil. "You got caught? Boy, you guys must be getting old or something."

Bruno winced. "Don't say that, okay?"

"I love it when you get put on dishwashing duty," Phil went on. "You've both got so much experience. I mean, you know exactly how to scrape the plates and load the machine. You're a couple of pros."

"Thanks, I think," said Bruno, accepting the hairnet that all kitchen workers had to wear. "Hey, Phil, just for old times' sake, how about you let us work without these things?"

"No can do, buddy. School rules. Okay, here come some trays. It's show time."

Bruno and Boots set to work, scraping and stacking. In minutes, they were bathed in sweat from the heat of the kitchen.

"Hello, suckers. Nice hair."

Both boys looked up. There, his head sticking through the tray window above the conveyor belt, was Edward O'Neal.

"Suckers?" repeated Boots. "You were at Scrimmage's, too. We could have ratted you out to the Fish, but we didn't. You're welcome."

Edward placed his tray on the belt. "My plate is especially dirty tonight," he informed them. "So you're going to have to put a little extra muscle into scraping off the hardened gravy and the fossilized mashed potatoes."

"Get him out of here," said Bruno without looking up, "or he's going through the pot-scrubber cycle."

Suddenly, Phil's voice rang out in the kitchen. "What the — ?"

Bruno and Boots wheeled. The assistant kitchen chief was crouched in front of the big industrial dishwasher, trying to stop a wall of suds. The white soapy froth was pouring through the steam vents, from the bottom and out of the gasket around the door. Phil backed up as it advanced.

Bruno and Boots waded into the bubbles.

"I'll turn it off!" called Bruno.

"*No!*" shrieked Phil. "You don't stand in water and touch an electrical switch!"

"Then what do we do?" called Boots. The suds were waist-deep and still coming.

"Get some help!" cried Phil, his voice muffled as he tried to clear a path through the suds.

"*Fi-i-i-i-re!*" howled Bruno.

Instantly, the chef and his crew stampeded onto the scene.

"What fire?" the chef demanded. "There's no fire!"

"Yeah!" cried Bruno. "But you wouldn't have come if I yelled 'bubbles!'"

The chef marched to the dry end of the kitchen, opened a fuse box, and flipped a circuit breaker. All at once, the lights went out, and the dishwasher fell silent. The mountain of suds began to settle slowly with the whispering sound made by popping bubbles.

The chef looked around the room with blazing eyes. "This doesn't just happen by accident! There must have been a box of detergent in that dishwasher! Now, who put it there?"

There was dead silence as suspicious glances darted like laser beams around the kitchen. Finally, all eyes came to rest on Bruno and Boots.

"What's everyone looking at us for?" Bruno demanded, outraged.

Phil frowned thoughtfully. "It's kind of a coincidence that this happens right when the two biggest practical jokers in the school are washing dishes."

"But we didn't do it!" squeaked Boots.

It took an extra hour to clean up the kitchen after dinner that evening. Bruno and Boots were there for every mop stroke and squeegee. The dirty looks from the kitchen staff didn't make things any more pleasant. No one seemed to believe that the caper had not been their doing.

"This year is really starting to get on my nerves," said Bruno, wringing his rag into a plastic pail. "First I meet your lousy brother, then the Fish shows up on a cane and now this. What idiot pulls a stupid stunt like this?"

Boots laughed mirthlessly. "Us, if we'd thought of it first. It was pretty funny."

"It's only funny when you don't have to clean it up," muttered Bruno. "If I ever get my hands on the kid who did this, he's a goner!"

Boots picked up a sponge to wipe off the counter. He paused. There, in a small puddle on the Formica, was a single brown feather. "Yeccch! What do they do — pluck the chickens right in here?"

"Either that or we drowned a pheasant," commented Bruno.

"It's not fair," said Boots feelingly. "They treat us like criminals over something that's not even our fault, while they run this kitchen like a pigsty."

"Life isn't fair," agreed Bruno. "Not this year, anyway."

* * *

"Mark!" Bruno Walton pounded on the door of room 114 in Dormitory 1. It was Friday morning, and this week's *Macdonald Hall Student Times* had just hit the stands. *"Mark!"*

The door opened, and Sidney Rampulsky, Mark's

roommate, peered out. "Hey, Bruno — Boots. What's all the yelling about? What do you guys want?"

"Mark Davies's head!" bellowed Bruno, elbowing his way into the room.

Mark looked over from his desk. "What's up?"

Bruno shoved his copy of the *Student Times* right under Mark's nose. A banner headline blazoned: *KITCHEN SOAP-O-RAMA*.

Underneath was a large picture of a soaked Bruno and Boots, waist-deep in suds.

Sidney leaned his elbow on Mark's desk, and moved in for a closer look. "You guys should have taken the hairnets off for the picture," he observed.

"We didn't exactly pose for it," said Boots bitterly.

"What's the big deal?" asked Mark. "I had to write about it. It's news."

Savagely, Bruno pointed to the bottom of the page, where the last two sentences were circled in Magic Marker:

The identity of the practical joker is not known. Bruno Walton and Melvin O'Neal were on dishwashing duty at the time of the incident.

"That practically says we did it!" Bruno stormed.

"Didn't you?" put in Sidney.

"No!" exclaimed Boots.

"The article doesn't accuse you of anything," Mark said calmly. "It's just the facts."

"Oh, sure," said Bruno sarcastically. "Facts like 'Someone got punched out in room 114 today. Mark Davies lives there.'"

"We were hauled down to the office to see the Fish over this!" added Boots hotly. "He believed us, but we had to do some fast talking."

Mark was thoughtful. "Maybe I can put a retraction in next week's paper. You know, something like 'Bruno and Boots deny all responsibility . . .'"

"That's even worse!" Boots protested. "It sounds like we're weaseling out of something!"

Sidney's elbow slid out from under him, and he whacked his jaw on the edge of the desk. He teetered for a moment, then shook his head to clear it. "Hey, if you guys didn't do it — who did?"

"How should we know?" growled Bruno. "Just because we didn't do it doesn't mean we know who did!"

He was still seething as he and Boots walked across the campus toward the Faculty Building and their classes.

As usual, Boots's anger dissipated first. "Don't you think you were a little hard on Mark? I mean, he is one of our closest friends."

"Hah!" sneered Bruno. "No true friend would ever publish a picture of a guy in a hairnet!"

A bustling figure crossed their path, almost sideswiping them.

Bruno recognized the crew cut first. "Hey, Elm, what's the hurry?"

Elmer stopped and stood there before them, hugging a brown paper parcel to his chest. "I – I have to take this to the mailbox — r–right away!"

"Another experiment for the museum to analyze?" asked Boots.

Elmer turned beet-red. "Not exactly. It's — personal."

Bruno caught sight of the address on the parcel. "*Marylou Beakman*," he read. He broke into a broad grin. "That's that girl you like. Way to go, Elm. I never thought you had the guts."

Elmer looked like he wanted to crawl into a hole.

"It's just — uh — a small — uh — gift — "

"Elmer, you blow me away," said Boots sincerely.

"What is it?" Bruno prompted. "Candy? A locket?"

"A rodent skull," replied Elmer. Bruno and Boots gaped. They were silent for so long that Elmer's face fell. "You think it's a bad present, don't you?"

"No!" cried Bruno, racking his brain for a response that wouldn't hurt Elmer's feelings. "It's just that, well — uh — maybe she's already got one."

"Oh, that's unlikely," said Elmer. "This particular skull is the species *Ondatra cephalus* which is quite rare in North America."

"Wow," said Boots in a strangled voice. He, too, didn't want to hurt Elmer, but the effort to keep a straight face was becoming painful.

"The thing is," said Bruno carefully, "girls sometimes like presents that are kind of, you know, romantic."

Elmer nodded. "I was considering sending her a pair of Jamaican cockroaches. But I was worried they'd escape through the air holes in the box. If she received an empty package, she would be perplexed."

"Not half as perplexed as the people at the post office," said Boots, biting his tongue to keep from laughing out loud.

Bruno was determined to get through to his friend.

"Maybe you'd be better off with something along the lines of — well, let's say flowers."

"Oh, no," said Elmer seriously. "Remember, Marylou is a fellow scientist. She wouldn't be interested in frivolous presents."

"I guess," said Bruno dubiously. "And when she sees the name Elmer Drimsdale — "

"Oh, I didn't sign the note," Elmer interrupted. "She doesn't know my name."

"Then how will she know who to — uh, thank?" asked Boots.

"I signed my number from the Summer Science Fair," said Elmer. "That's how she'd remember me." He looked around nervously. "I've got to hurry, or I'll miss the mail pickup."

Bruno and Boots were silent as he scampered away. By unspoken agreement, they ducked into the Faculty Building washroom, and burst into howls of laughter, leaning on each other for support.

* * *

"*Dear Mom,*" read Diane. "*How are you? I am fine. School is great.*" She looked up. "What else is there to say?"

Cathy lay on her bed, tossing a football into the air, and catching it with sure hands. "How about 'Bruno tried to strangle Boots's kid brother.'"

Diane laughed. "I wish I could put that. It would make a more interesting letter."

"Edward's a cute little guy," Cathy reflected. "A bit on the crazy side — "

A sudden scream echoed through the hallway. In a flash, Cathy and Diane were out their door and down the hall to the source of the cry. They found Marylou Beakman in her corner room, staring into an open box.

"What's wrong?" Cathy demanded.

Marylou was backing away from the box, pointing. "It — it came in today's mail!"

Cathy and Diane leaned over to take a look. There, packaged in bubble wrap, was a small bleached skull. "Cool!" said Cathy. "A voodoo curse!"

Marylou screamed again.

Diane made a face. "It looks like some small animal."

"But who would send it?" quavered Marylou. "And why would they send it to *me*?"

Miss Scrimmage burst into the room. "Now, now, what's the disturbance?"

Cathy pointed to the box. "Somebody put a curse on Marylou."

The Headmistress smiled tolerantly. "You girls have such vivid imaginations. Of course, you know there is no such thing as — " She caught sight of the skull and went deathly pale. "What — what — ?"

Cathy and Diane eased her into the chair and began fanning her with a pillowcase.

"Oh, thank you, girls!" breathed Miss Scrimmage. "I'm fine. Now, Catherine — Diane — please leave us so that Marylou and I can have a little chat."

Reluctantly, Cathy and Diane left the room, shutting the door behind them.

Miss Scrimmage turned to Marylou. "Now, dear, tell me what you know of this."

"It came in today's mail," the distressed girl explained. "It's so creepy!"

Bravely, like she was putting her hands into piranha-infested waters, Miss Scrimmage riffled through the box, and pulled out a note.

Dear Marylou,

I know you, of all people, will appreciate this.

#57

"Aha!" said Miss Scrimmage in triumph. "The culprit was foolish enough to leave us a big, fat clue to his identity!"

"Fifty-seven?" repeated Marylou in confusion.

"Now, you must mention this to no one," instructed Miss Scrimmage, examining the wrapping for a return address. "I don't want the girls to become alarmed — " All at once, she sucked in her breath in a gasp. The package was from Macdonald Hall.

Chapter 4

tyrannosaurus rex

Mr. Sturgeon entered his cottage and dropped his cane into an umbrella stand near the door.

"Mildred!" he called.

"I'm in the kitchen, dear. Would you like some tea?"

The Headmaster limped through the swinging door, and joined his wife at the table. "Perhaps I shouldn't tell you now," he mused, biting into a tea biscuit. "I ought to wait until you are trying to convince me, for the umpteenth time, that Miss Scrimmage is not as crazy as a bedbug. Then I could pull out this trump card, and settle the issue once and for all."

Mrs. Sturgeon poured his tea. "William, whatever are you talking about?"

"I took a call from Miss Scrimmage late this afternoon," said the Headmaster. "She claims that a Macdonald Hall student has placed a voodoo curse on one of her young ladies."

His wife gawked. "Surely she's joking, William! Or it's revenge for the dreadful way you treated her last week."

"I thought so, too, Mildred. And I attempted to dismiss her in my usual way. But she is adamant. And now I find myself in the bizarre position of searching for a witch doctor."

"Just how are you expected to do that?" his wife inquired.

"With her big clue, obviously. She says the culprit signed his note with the number fifty-seven. I explained that our student numbers have four digits, and she threatened to sue me for obstruction of justice. Have you ever heard the like?"

Mrs. Sturgeon chuckled. "Well, you must admit your life isn't a 'no-brainer' anymore. This is the challenge you wanted."

"It isn't a challenge," her husband countered. "This is lunacy from Miss Scrimmage. It happens every year."

"Well, what about those strange events going on at our school?" she persisted. "Your usual jokers, Bruno and Melvin, have nothing to do with them."

"So *they* say," said Mr. Sturgeon cynically. "I wonder if I'm not being a little gullible to trust their word."

* * *

"Sorry I'm late, Coach," puffed Boots, who had run all the way across the campus to the pool building.

Coach Flynn frowned at him. "If you want to stay on the

swim team, O'Neal, remember that practice starts on the dot."

"Sorry," Boots said again. "My mom called, and she talked my ear off about my kid brother, Edward."

"Did you tell her how weird he is?" asked Pete Anderson, tying the string of his bathing suit.

Boots opened his locker. "She knows that. She's his mother, after all." He groaned. "She wants me to make sure the little monster's doing okay in his classes. Just what I needed — a part-time job as a nanny!"

"What a strange dude!" put in Sidney. "The word around our dorm is he's constantly sneaking in and out in the middle of the night."

Boots held his head. "Oh, great. My brother, the juvenile delinquent."

"Kind of like you and Bruno *your* first year here," observed Pete.

The coach clapped his hands. "All right, let's go, men." He led the team out into the pool area.

Boots stepped into his suit, and scrambled after his teammates. He was a dozen strides from the edge of the pool when the others began to jump in. He sprinted across the tile apron — and froze —

The other swimmers hit the water, touched bottom, sprang up again and broke the surface — bright blue!

"What the — ?" bellowed Coach Flynn.

"What's wrong?" asked Sidney, flipping the wet hair out of his eyes. He caught sight of his hand. "I'm blue!"

Boots hung back in dismay. What was going on here? Something in the water was turning skin blue!

"Everybody out of the pool!" bellowed Flynn.

There was much splashing and shouting as seven blue bodies heaved themselves up over the side.

* * *

Bruno strolled across the campus on his way to meet Boots at the pool building. Bruno himself didn't know how to swim, but he always liked to watch the team work out.

He was just going up the walk when the door burst open, and out paraded the Macdonald Hall swim team, in all their baby-blue glory. Their lips were purple; their hair ranged from turquoise to deep indigo. Pete, who was the blondest of them, sported bright-green curls.

Bruno gaped. "What happened?"

"As if you don't know!" seethed Sidney.

The group stomped past, eyes shooting sparks.

"Big joke!"

"I'll get you for this!"

"When are you idiots going to grow up?"

Pete was bringing up the rear. "This time you've gone too far! How about remembering who your friends are?"

Speechless, Bruno watched them storm off. Then he turned and ran into the building. Boots and Coach Flynn were the only ones in the pool area.

"This may sound stupid," said Bruno, "but I just saw a whole bunch of really crabby blue people!"

Flynn glared at him. "Walton. I should have guessed you'd turn up here to have a look at your handiwork. Well, I'm going to report this."

"But, sir," protested Boots, "we didn't do it!"

"Do you think I'm an idiot?" cried the coach. "Everybody jumped in — except you! You *knew* there was blue dye in the water!" He pointed at Bruno. "And guess who's the first spectator that happens to drop in? Well, this wasn't funny!" He marched into the locker room, fuming.

Bruno knelt and dipped his fingertip into the water. It came out blue. "Pretty good joke," he admitted grudgingly.

"This is getting serious," said Boots in alarm. "All those gags we pulled over the years are coming back to haunt us. If an ant sneezes on the east lawn, everybody comes straight to us! Even our best friends think we're guilty, Bruno . . . Bruno?"

Bruno was bent over the diving board, examining something with great interest. "Come here, Boots. Take a look at this."

Boots joined him. There on the springboard sat a neat brown feather. He shrugged. "So?"

"So did we or did we not find one of these in the kitchen the day the dishwasher overflowed?"

"We did!" Boots breathed. "What could it mean?"

Bruno put the feather in his shirt pocket. "I have a theory."

* * *

Bruno and Boots rushed past the dormitories to the Faculty Building and the statue of Sir John A. Macdonald out in front of it.

"It's been over a week," Boots panted. "It could have blown away, or been chopped up by the lawnmowers. Maybe it was never there at all."

"There's only one way to find out," said Bruno. He dropped down to all fours and began to comb the grass with his fingers. Boots did the same.

They searched diligently, going through the lawn almost blade by blade.

"Paydirt!" exclaimed Bruno suddenly.

Boots scrambled over. Tangled in the untrimmed grass around some bushes a few metres from the statue was a small brown feather.

Bruno pulled the pool feather from his pocket and held it up against the new finding.

"Perfect match," Boots commented.

Bruno nodded. "There's no doubt in my mind that this was left here when the scuba suit went on Sir John A. It's a calling card."

Boots looked blank. "What are you talking about? Whose calling card?"

"The guy who rigged the scuba suit and the dishwasher and the pool." He regarded the matched feathers in his hand. "Face it, Boots — we've got a phantom practical joker on the loose at Macdonald Hall!"

* * *

Miss Scrimmage stood on the stage in the school gym and looked out over the assembled student body. "Now, girls, I don't want to alarm anybody, but I think it's time we had a discussion about" — she shuddered at the mere thought — "security."

There was an uneasy murmur, and the Headmistress held up her hands for quiet. "Macdonald Hall students have been involved in unsavoury incidents tormenting us — that is nothing new. But now one of our young ladies has received a threatening package from one of those marauders across the road — it is too horrible for me to mention — " She uncorked a vial of smelling salts and inhaled deeply.

"But Miss Scrimmage," called out Cathy from the fourth

row. "You've always done such a great job protecting us with your shotgun! We feel totally safe!" A chorus of cheers backed up her statement.

"Thank you, Catherine — girls," said Miss Scrimmage, a little choked up from this show of support. "However, I feel that I can no longer shoulder the burden alone. That is why I've called you here today — to introduce you to our new watchdog, Rex."

"Great," whispered Cathy. "We're getting a puppy."

Diane was nervous. "Cathy, when you need a dog for security, I don't think they sell you a cute, cuddly one."

"Aw, come on," grinned Cathy. "Knowing Miss Scrimmage, she probably bought an attack poodle." A fit of giggles was interrupted by a bark that was more of a roar. An enormous animal bounded onto the stage, dragging Miss Smedley, the gym teacher, on the end of a leather leash. There was a gasp from the student body.

"Please welcome our new little helper," beamed the Headmistress, in spite of the fact that the black Doberman stood nearly as tall as she did. "One look at Rex, and the boys of Macdonald Hall should, as they say, run a mile."

"One look at Rex and an M-1 tank would run a mile," breathed Diane in terror.

"Oh, don't be such a wimp," laughed Cathy. "I grew up with big dogs. Their bark is worse than their bite. Watch this!" She put her forefingers in her mouth and emitted a sharp whistle.

Rex's pointy ears perked up like a radar. His lean, black body tensed, then sprang, sending Miss Smedley flying. She had to let go of the leash to avoid being pulled off the stage.

There were screams as Rex hurled himself over the first three rows in a single leap and landed with his front paws on Cathy's knees. Teeth bared, he held that pose, ready to pounce.

Miss Scrimmage pulled a small whistle from the pocket of her skirt and blew. Obediently, Rex trotted back up the steps to the stage. He looked defiantly out at the crowd, snarling.

Slowly, Cathy allowed herself to start breathing again. Diane removed her iron grip on her roommate's arm.

"Isn't he wonderful?" declared the Headmistress, pleased. "Thank you, Catherine, for assisting with that demonstration. Now, Miss Smedley — Miss Smedley? Girls, would someone please help Miss Smedley?"

The gym teacher was still sprawled out on the steps, her face frozen in terror.

"Cathy, are you okay?" whispered Diane as the front row set about reviving Miss Smedley.

"Now I know why his name is Rex," said Cathy in awe. "It's shortened — from Tyrannosaurus!"

Chapter 5

the prime suspects

"So wherever this guy plays a gag he leaves a feather?"

It was nine o'clock, but Boots couldn't concentrate on his homework. The phantom practical joker was on his mind.

"It's like a trademark," said Bruno. "In the movies, all the master criminals leave a card or a glove at the scene of the crime. I saw one flick where this safecracker put live toads in the vault after cleaning out the money."

Boots groaned. "Bruno, putting a scuba suit on a statue hardly makes a guy a master criminal."

"But it works the same way," Bruno insisted. "Whether it's live toads or feathers, it's like a signature. The criminal is daring the cops to catch him. Or, with our phantom, daring the Fish."

"Yeah, but the only suspects the Fish has are us," Boots complained. "*We're* the ones who get called to the office every time the Phantom pulls something." He slammed his math book shut. "After all the stuff we've gotten away with, do you realize that we might get suspended for something that's not even our fault?"

Bruno threw himself backwards onto his bed. "I thought of that," he said slowly. "And there's only one thing to do."

"Change schools?" Boots asked miserably.

"We're going to catch the Phantom ourselves and bring him to justice," Bruno announced.

Boots goggled. "Catch him? Are you out of your mind?"

Bruno rolled his eyes. "Well, Melvin, our only other choice is to sit on our butts and take the heat for what the Phantom does."

"Oh, shut up!" Boots said in disgust. "I'd love to stop this kid just as much as you. The problem is we don't know who he is."

"Think," Bruno said with determination. "Who would be capable of pulling all this Phantom stuff?" He added, "Besides us, I mean."

The two boys sat in silence, racking their brains. All at once, they both leapt to their feet.

"*Edward!*" they chorused.

"Of course!" said Boots breathlessly. "He wants to show us up!"

"And he's been sneaking out at night!" added Bruno.

"He says we're over the hill old men and he's the new generation," Boots went on. "He thinks he's replacing us by out joking us."

Bruno punched his fist in the air. "Let's go kill him."

Boots put an iron grip on his arm. "We can't. Not unless we're one hundred percent positive it's Edward."

Bruno sat back down. "Think of all the guys we know. Who else could be the Phantom?"

"Well," Boots began slowly. "Maybe none of the guys could pull off those stunts, but — "

Bruno snapped his fingers. "Cathy! Cathy and Diane!"

"Cathy could do it with one hand tied behind her back!" added Boots.

Bruno shook his head. "It doesn't make sense. How could Cathy and Diane be the Phantom? They haven't been on Macdonald Hall property all year."

"How do you know that?" asked Boots.

Bruno shrugged. "They're our friends. If they were here, they would have dropped by our room to say hi, right?"

"Unless," said Boots, "they're avoiding us, because they don't want us to find out they're the Phantom."

There was a long pause, as the two pondered this.

At last, Bruno spoke. "This is getting more complicated than I thought. Okay, it might be Cathy and Diane, and that explains why they haven't come by. If it's not them, it's Edward — "

"Right," confirmed Boots. He frowned. "But if my brother's the Phantom, what's been keeping the girls away?"

* * *

It was after midnight when Cathy swung a leg over the sill of her room at Miss Scrimmage's Finishing School for Young Ladies. She looked back at Diane, who was cowering by the window. "What's your problem?"

Diane's voice was haunted. "*He's* out there somewhere. I know it."

"Don't be such a baby," laughed Cathy. "Let's go. Bruno and Boots probably think we've died."

"They might be right," Diane muttered, easing herself out the window.

The two girls were halfway down the drainpipe when the barking began. It seemed to be coming from the apple orchard, but the echoes surrounded them.

"Tyrannosaurus Rex!" squeaked Diane in terror.

The big Doberman burst into the clearing and stopped on a dime under the downspout, growling and drooling up at them.

Diane tried to shinny back up to the room, but Cathy grabbed her ankle and held her back.

"Relax, Diane. I've thought of everything." From her jacket pocket, Cathy produced a lumpy package covered in tin foil. Carefully, she peeled off the wrapping to reveal a large lump of ground beef. This she held out toward Rex. "Take a whiff of this, you carnivorous mutt," she called softly. "Raw meat. Your favourite." To Diane she whispered, "Get ready to run for it."

"But, Cathy — "

Before Diane could protest, Cathy lobbed the hamburger toward the apple orchard. Rex took off after the flying meat.

"Now!" Cathy hauled Diane down the drainpipe, and the two sprinted for the wrought-iron fence.

Out of the corner of their eyes, the fleeing girls caught sight of Rex leaping straight up in the air, catching the meat and wolfing it down in a single gulp. There was no way they could make it to the fence before the Doberman came after them.

"Retreat!" hissed Cathy.

At that, she was a good three steps behind Diane in the race back to their window. Cathy hit the drainpipe climbing, but not before Rex's powerful jaws had removed five centimetres from the cuff of her jeans.

Once in the room, the two stood panting while Rex clawed the drainpipe and barked up at them.

"He really is a Tyrannosaurus rex!" breathed Cathy in awe. "That was half a *kilo* of hamburger! He didn't eat it; he *inhaled* it!"

"That's nothing!" gasped Diane. "I saw Miss Scrimmage feeding him today! He cleaned out his dish and then attacked the bag! Miss Smedley's still in shock!"

Cathy sat down on her bed, frowning. "Man, this stinks. We can't get over to see Bruno and Boots. For all we know, Macdonald Hall might have burned to the ground and that's an empty shell standing across the road! The guys are probably mixed up in all kinds of cool stuff by now and we're missing it!"

Diane shrugged. "What choice do we have? Tyrannosaurus Rex is an eating machine! He'll eat anything and lots of it."

"You're right," Cathy said glumly. Suddenly, a fiendish grin spread itself across her fair features. "Yeah! You're right!"

Diane was cautious. "I don't like that look on your face."

"He'll eat anything!" Cathy repeated." And it's our job to see that he gets it. Starting tomorrow, we're waitresses!"

Diane was mystified. "Who are we waiting on?

"One great, big, nasty, ugly Tyrannosaurus Rex."

Chapter 6

niagara falls

Edward O'Neal was shooting baskets alone in the gym when his shot was suddenly blocked by a high-reaching hand.

His older brother Boots grabbed the ball out of the air and rolled it into the equipment room. "I've been looking all over for you."

"I wasn't 'all over,'" said Edward. "I was here."

"The word is you're here a lot," said Boots. His eyes narrowed. "When you're not sneaking out in the middle of the night. Ever do any work?"

"What's it to you?"

Boots frowned. "Look, Edward. Personally, I don't care if you finish up the year with a zero percent average. But

Mom has already promised me a very un-merry Christmas if you flunk out."

"I'm not going to flunk!" blustered Edward.

"Not even math?"

The younger boy was startled. "How do you know about math?"

Boots shrugged expansively. "Mom is like the CIA. She's got all our weaknesses on file."

Edward shuffled uncomfortably. "Okay, I've had a few problems with math. But I'm taking care of them. Don't worry, I won't ruin your Christmas."

"Good," Boots nodded. "Because if I have a bad holiday, yours is going to be worse."

* * *

Miss Scrimmage sat at the head table in the pink and silver dining room, picking daintily at her lunch. She always made a point of eating with her students. That way she could coach them on those subtle matters of etiquette — the proper way to hold a pickle fork or to dab at one's mouth with a linen napkin. Some of the parents called her old-fashioned, but that didn't bother Miss Scrimmage. One day, she knew, her young ladies might be called upon to eat a piece of corn on the cob in the presence of kings, presidents and prime ministers. Her girls would be ready.

"Catherine, Diane!" She stopped them at the door. "Why on earth are you carrying such enormous parcels?"

Cathy shifted her weight under the jam-packed green garbage bag of food she was hefting. "Just a little snack to get me through the afternoon."

"We're always starving by dinnertime," put in Diane, struggling with her own supplies.

"But why so *much?*" Miss Scrimmage peeked inside Cathy's parcel. It contained cold cuts, a slab of lasagna, Salisbury steak, potato chips, an assortment of cookies and cupcakes and almost half of a lemon meringue pie. "These foods are so high in fat! Haven't you been paying attention in Miss Smedley's health class?"

"We're doing square dancing in phys. ed.," said Cathy airily. "It burns a zillion calories." And she headed off with her burden.

Miss Scrimmage watched as Cathy and Diane were followed by a long procession. Each of the girls was just as loaded down with leftovers as Cathy. She frowned. Afternoon snacks. How odd!

* * *

"Wow, look at him eat!" breathed Ruth Sidwell in awe.

A crowd of girls were packed into the equipment room off the gym watching Rex devour mountains of leftovers from lunch.

"*We're* probably next," said Diane nervously.

Wilma Dorf looked perplexed. "I don't get it. Isn't he going to get fat if we keep feeding him like this?"

Cathy looked at her pityingly. "That's the whole point, Wilma. We're going to take this lean, mean killing machine and turn him into a chubby, slow, happy, paunchy pooch. This Tyrannosaurus's life is going to be suppertime, naptime, suppertime, naptime. Got it?"

Ruth nodded. "If he's always eating and sleeping, he can't be mauling any of us."

Diane was unconvinced. "He doesn't look like he's ready to roll over and fall asleep. He looks like he's ready for another seventeen lemon meringue pies."

On cue, Rex inhaled the last of the pie and turned his attention to a stack of sliced bologna.

"Rome wasn't built in a day," lectured Cathy. "Let's hope the cafeteria has plenty of doggy bags. Prepare for a canine smorgasbord!"

* * *

First period math class had been going on for about ten minutes when Boots happened to glance up. Bright colours caught his eye. That's when he looked to the ceiling and saw the dozens of water balloons hanging above them.

He nudged Wilbur in the desk beside him. "*Pssst*," he whispered, pointing his index finger straight up.

Wilbur craned his neck. "Whoa!"

Sidney followed Wilbur's gaze and turned pale. "How did those get up there?" he hissed.

Three pairs of eyes traced the long white strings that stretched from the dangling water balloons to the class-room door.

"Uh-oh," said Wilbur. "You don't suppose it's hooked up so that, when the door opens, all the balloons fall — "

"We're trapped!" managed Sidney in agony.

"O'Neal, Hackenschleimer, Rampulsky — " Mr. Stratton said sternly. "Would you care to let the whole class in on your conversation?"

Boots swallowed hard. "Sorry, sir, but we couldn't help noticing all those, uh, water balloons on the ceiling, and — "

The teacher looked up. "Good Lord!" he blurted, jumping back as though jolted with a severe electric shock. "All right, nobody panic! We shall proceed out the door in an orderly — "

"Not the door!" bellowed Wilbur. "That'll drop the balloons!"

"The window!" cried Sidney, and led the stampede for the front of the room. Unfortunately, he tripped over a desk leg and crashed to the floor, blocking the way.

There was a polite knock at the door. "Mr. Stratton?" called Larry Wilson from the hall.

"No-o-o!" It came from at least a dozen throats.

Larry opened the door, tugging on the series of strings. By the time the office messenger peered inside, water balloons were raining down from the ceiling, exploding on Mr. Stratton and his hapless students.

"What'd I do?" asked Larry, mystified.

And as the drenched class filed out of the room to change into dry clothes, Boots saw it. It was floating in a small puddle just inside the doorway: another brown feather.

* * *

"Sorry about that, Boots," Larry was saying as he walked across the campus with Bruno and Boots. "I just opened the door and all of a sudden, Niagara Falls!"

"Don't sweat it, Larry," Bruno assured him. "We know it wasn't you. It was the Phantom."

Larry stared at him. "The who?"

"There's a phantom practical joker at Macdonald Hall. He's the guy who's been pulling all this stuff."

"Yeah, well I'm pretty sure the Fish thinks it's *us*," Boots said bitterly. "Why else would we be called to his office again?"

"Hey, Larry," said Bruno as they entered the Faculty Building. "What have you found out about the Fish and his cane and all that?"

"All he'll say is that it's medical," Larry replied in a low voice. "But I overheard him on the phone talking about an operation."

"I knew it!" exclaimed Bruno. "The Fish is really sick!"

"What kind of operation?" asked Boots.

Larry shook his head. "No idea. Okay, you guys can go in now."

* * *

Mr. Sturgeon leaned across his desk and fixed Bruno and Boots with his best fishy stare. "I received a call from our gardener today. The man was hysterical. He insisted there were apples growing on the oak trees. It turned out they were tied on with wire. Also, in the kitchen, the toasters had been loaded with bread, turned on their sides, and connected so that all six would pop the instant the door was opened. Our kitchen staff was shot with toast this morning. In addition, there was an incident involving water balloons with which I believe you, O'Neal, are familiar." The Headmaster leaned back in his chair. "The entire campus is buzzing with these stories, and two names are being bandied about as the probable culprits: Walton and O'Neal."

Bruno spoke up. "Sir, we have reason to believe that this is all the work of a phantom practical joker."

Mr. Sturgeon seemed unimpressed. "But is it the work of a phantom practical joker named Walton?" He turned to Boots. "Or O'Neal?"

Boots's reply was earnest. "Sir, we weren't lying before, and we aren't lying now."

The Headmaster paused. Should he ask about Miss Scrimmage's voodoo curse? He frowned. That would be unfair. Walton and O'Neal had always been mischievous, but never had they been involved in anything related to the occult. And they certainly couldn't be held responsible for Miss Scrimmage's insane imagination.

"Very well," he said finally. "But I must warn you boys. I do not give my trust lightly. And if it is misplaced here, things will go very, very hard for you. Is that clear?"

"Yes, sir," chorused Bruno and Boots.

* * *

Heading back for Dormitory 3, the boys ran into Elmer Drimsdale. The school genius was on his way to the mail drop, hugging a small package to his chest.

"What have you got there, Elm?" Bruno greeted. "More stuff for your girlfriend?"

Elmer flushed. "Marylou Beakman is obviously a very shy person. I haven't heard anything from her about my first present."

"Maybe she was speechless when she got the rodent skull," Boots suggested.

"Well, this time I'm taking your advice, Bruno," Elmer declared. "I'm sending her something so spectacular she'll have to sit up and take notice."

Bruno regarded the little box critically. "Jewellery, right? Gee, Elm, I hope you didn't spend too much — "

Elmer waved his hand impatiently. "Nothing as shallow and mindless as that! I'm giving a rare and invaluable gift."

Both boys looked at him expectantly.

Elmer motioned them closer, as though he were about to share top-secret, classified information. "Last week I came into possession of a small sample of the droppings of the Tasmanian Mountain Sparrow."

"Yeah, but what's the present?" asked Bruno.

"I'm sending her half of my specimen," Elmer said proudly.

It took a moment for this to sink in.

"You're giving her *droppings?*" asked Boots in disbelief.

"*Bird* droppings?" added Bruno.

"The droppings of the Tasmanian Mountain Sparrow are the most nutrient-rich of any species of bird in the world!" Elmer crowed gleefully. "The opportunities for study will be limitless. Not to mention how difficult this specimen is to come by in the northern hemisphere. This is one present Marylou will never forget!"

"You can say that again," put in Boots.

"Say, Elm," Bruno began carefully. "Are you sure that Marylou is as big on science as you are? If she is — great! She'll love it. But if she isn't — well, getting bird droppings in the mail could be kind of a turnoff for some girls."

"I've thought of that," Elmer told them. "And that's why I've included a thorough explanation of exactly what the specimen is." He glanced at his watch. "I have to hurry. I want to catch today's mail pickup." And he rushed off, cradling his package.

"Something tells me this romance isn't going to work out," Boots commented dryly.

Bruno nodded. "Poor Elmer." He shrugged. "On the other hand, maybe Elmer's right and Marylou is really going to groove on this stuff — "

Bruno and Boots looked at each other thoughtfully. "Nah!" they chorused, and walked off, laughing.

* * *

Bruno and Boots were just drifting off to sleep that night, when a frantic scratching at the window disturbed them.

"I'll bet it's Cathy and Diane," yawned Bruno. "It's about time they came over to see us."

Boots threw open the window, and both boys peered out. There, hopelessly entangled in the honeysuckle hushes, lay Sidney Rampulsky.

"Sidney! What are you doing here?" whispered Boots, reaching out an arm.

Sidney took Boots's outstretched arm and hoisted himself over the sill into the room. "You said to keep an eye on Edward," he replied breathlessly. "Well, he just snuck out of our dorm."

Bruno clapped his hands together with determination. "Tonight we nail the Phantom! Where'd he go?"

Sidney looked blank. "How should I know? As soon as I saw him leave I came over here."

The three scrambled out the window and scanned the darkened campus. Boots, who had the best night sight, spied their quarry first. Edward O'Neal, dressed in black, was making his way across the campus.

"Don't lose him," hissed Bruno as they followed from a safe distance. "I can't wait to catch your brother and take his Phantom feathers and stick them up his nose one at a time."

Boots squinted into the gloom. Edward was scampering for the highway. "He's headed for Scrimmage's!"

"I thought the Phantom only struck at Macdonald Hall," put in Sidney.

"Come on," said Bruno grimly. "Let's follow him."

"Aw, Bruno!" Boots complained. "Even if he *is* the

Phantom, he's not phantoming tonight. Let's just go back to sleep."

But Bruno was already starting for the road. "Our biggest suspects are Edward and Cathy," he lectured. "If they're meeting tonight, I want to get to the bottom of it. Maybe it's a conspiracy."

Boots and Sidney exchanged helpless shrugs, and darted after Bruno. There was a brief moment of panic when Sidney fell off the wrought-iron fence surrounding Miss Scrimmage's school, but he was only winded, and the chase resumed.

"Wait a minute," whispered Boots. "He's not going to Cathy and Diane's room."

It was true. Edward passed right underneath the girls' window and continued on behind the school.

The three boys sped up to a run, and quickly closed the gap behind Edward. Boots reached out and spun his brother around.

Edward looked first shocked and then disgusted. "Would you two old men do me a favour and get a life?" He turned his gaze on Sidney, who was caked with grass and dirt, and wild-eyed from his spill off the fence. "Let me guess. You were drilling for oil with your face."

Sidney just stared.

"What if I wrote Mom that you've been coming over here?" Boots raged.

"Are you going to tell her that you caught me personally?" Edward asked innocently.

Bruno looked at his watch. "As much as I'd love to hang out here and talk with this insect, I vote for a visit to Cathy and Diane. We haven't seen them since the first day — and that time, something real ugly came up." He glared at Edward.

Boots sighed heavily. "Let's just get out of here before we all end up in trouble."

No sooner were the words out of his mouth, than there was a low growling sound, and a large, dark shape appeared from the front of the school. Rex swaggered into the clearing, his Doberman features becoming clearer in the moonlight. The big animal squinted at them through cruel eyes that were little more than slits.

"I wonder whose dog it is," mused Boots.

"He's not a dog; he's a Tyrannosaurus rex!" came Diane's voice from above. "Miss Scrimmage bought him for protection!"

"Come on," scoffed Bruno. "*This* is what's been keeping you girls away? A little puppy?"

Cathy appeared at her side. "Don't mess with him, Bruno," she called down. "This is one evil mutt, no lie!"

"*Aha!*" shrilled a triumphant voice.

There, on a side balcony, stood Miss Scrimmage, wrapped in a frilly, pink dressing gown.

"Please, Miss Scrimmage!" cried Diane. "Punish them, and call Mr. Sturgeon, and make them promise never to come back, but please, *please*, call off Rex!"

But Miss Scrimmage was in her finest hour. "A lady may appear to be soft on the outside, Diane — but inside she is as strong as a bar of steel." She turned her attention to the four cornered, quaking boys. "You brutes have terrorized us for the last time! All right, Rex — sic '*em!*"

Rex barked, a roar that echoed off the trees. The boys jumped back, and Sidney tripped on a tree root. He went down heavily. The big Doberman took three menacing steps toward the group, then yawned hugely and curled up into a ball on the grass, fast asleep.

On the ground, Sidney had his hands over his eyes. "I can't look! What's happening?"

"I – I think that dog just died — " stammered Bruno.

Rex began to snore softly.

"He's not dead — he's asleep!" said Boots in disbelief.

"Asleep?!" Cathy practically jumped out her window with excitement. "That's us! We did it! A whole week of overfeeding, and it finally paid off!"

"Just in time to save the guys!" Diane added.

Miss Scrimmage was livid. "What have you done to my dog, you marauders, you terrorists, you hooligans?" she shrieked down at the Macdonald Hall boys.

Bruno summed up everyone's feelings: "*Ru-u-u-un!!*"

Cathy and Diane watched the footrace from their window.

"Wow," whistled Cathy. "Those guys should try out for the Olympics."

Chapter 7

marylou beakman hates me

PHANTOM JOKE SPREE PARALYZES SCHOOL blazoned the banner headline of the *Macdonald Hall Student Times.*

Widespread interest had prompted Mark to put out a special edition of the school paper devoted almost completely to the notorious Phantom. In fact, the only article not related to the practical jokes was, *REX TO BE PUT ON LOW CALORIE DIET UNTIL VICIOUS AGAIN, MISS SCRIMMAGE SAYS,* at the bottom of page four.

Mark was distributing papers in the dining hall at dinner, and they were going like hotcakes. Students jabbered excitedly about the gags they themselves had witnessed, and read with amazement of the others. Reaction ranged from anger to laughter to outright admiration for the master practical joker.

"I don't know whether to kill the guy or shake his hand," said Larry, engrossed in the paper. "Check this out:

> *On Wednesday, the Phantom reprogrammed the class-change bell to knock six minutes off each hour. At the end of eighth period, students and teachers were bewildered to find an entire period still to go, even though they had completed their full schedules."*

Sidney snapped his fingers. "I remember that. It was nuts. Everybody was packed into the hall, pushing and shoving and trying to figure out what we'd missed, and then somebody set off a smoke bomb!"

"*Somebody* my foot," snarled Bruno. "It was the Phantom."

"I thought you'd *like* the Phantom," Sidney told Bruno. "I mean, he's exactly your style, and his stunts are brilliant. Half the guys think it's you and Boots."

"Well, it's not!" snapped Bruno testily.

"Listen to this one," put in Boots, skimming his own *Student Times.* "It says this guy dissected a frog for biology. Overnight, the Phantom took away the frog halves and replaced them with two new live frogs. And this poor kid did a whole science project on how frogs are like worms; when you cut them in half, the two parts go on living on their own."

Wilbur scowled over a stack of chicken cutlets. "Well, you can't blame the Phantom for a guy being stupid," he said in disgust. "I mean, what kind of an idiot thinks that frogs are like worms? Sheesh!"

"Wait a minute." Pete Anderson looked up from his plate. "That was me!" He peered at the paper over Boots's shoulder. "I knew that sounded familiar. Cool!" he declared. "I made the paper."

Wilbur rolled his eyes.

Bruno looked thoughtful. "Maybe we've been thinking about this whole thing the wrong way," he began slowly. "Maybe we should ask ourselves who stands to benefit the most from the Phantom?"

"Benefit?" mumbled Wilbur, his mouth full. "Who benefits from practical jokes?"

Bruno looked to the front of the dining hall where Mark was handing out papers. "Whose stupid newspaper that nobody cares about, let alone reads, is suddenly hot stuff now that he's got the Phantom to write about?"

Boots was the first to catch on. "You think Mark is the Phantom? And he's doing it to create good stories for the *Student Times?*"

Sidney spoke up. "He *does* always complain that nobody takes much of an interest in the paper," he said breathlessly.

Bruno nodded sagely. "And that makes Mark the prime suspect."

Sidney looked up from his plate. "I thought Edward was the prime suspect."

"That was Cathy," Pete corrected. "*She's* the prime suspect."

"They're all suspects," said Bruno definitely.

"Aw, come on, Bruno!" Boots exploded. "There's no way we can watch all of them at the same time."

"It depends what you mean by 'we,'" said Bruno cheerfully. "You and I can't do it all. But when you throw in Wilbur, Larry, Pete, Sidney — "

"Hold it." Wilbur held up a meaty palm as though directing traffic. "I'm not spying on anybody."

"It's not spying," Bruno insisted. "It's surveillance."

"Surveillance?" repeated Pete. "What's that?"

"Spying," translated Larry. "Look, Bruno, maybe the Phantom's not so funny anymore, but that doesn't make him Jack the Ripper. We've got classes. We've got homework. We hang out with friends. We go to the rec hall every now and then. Sometimes we even sleep! We don't have time for surveillance."

Bruno set his jaw stubbornly. "Every time Boots and I tell the Fish we didn't do anything, he believes us a little less. One of these days we're going to end up suspended. And when the jokes don't stop, the Fish is going to go looking for somebody else — maybe even you."

There was a long silence while they all took in what seemed to be an undeniable truth.

"I'll take Mark," Sidney said finally. "After all, he's my roommate."

Big Wilbur caved in next. "Oh, all right," he mumbled. "Who's my assignment?"

"We'll draw up a schedule," said Bruno briskly. "Larry, you cover Mark when Sidney's not around. Wilbur and Pete switch off on Edward. Boots and I take Scrimmage's."

"This is crazy," Boots complained. "Cathy and Diane are our friends. Why can't we just go over there and ask them if they're behind these practical jokes?"

Bruno shook his head. "I know it's tough, but we're going to have to keep our distance from Cathy and Diane until we can prove they're not the Phantom."

"They probably don't know anything about it," Boots said sourly. "How could they, except from us?"

Bruno was adamant. "The only way to be sure is to watch them day and night."

"Day and night?" repeated Boots. "How can we do that? We don't live there, remember?"

"I've already thought of that," Bruno assured him. "If Cathy and Diane are pulling this Phantom stuff, they must be sneaking over to the Hall. So all we have to do is keep watch on the drainpipe outside their window. That's the only way for them to sneak out."

"No chance!" snapped Boots. "My parents didn't send me to the Hall to spend every night hunkered down in Miss Scrimmage's apple orchard, being eaten by mosquitoes, watching a stupid drainpipe!"

"We don't have to *go* there," said Bruno impatiently. "We can watch by telescope in the comfort of our own room."

"Telescope? What telescope?"

"Elmer's telescope," Bruno explained. "If it can pick up the Crab Nebula, surely it can reach as far as Scrimmage's." He looked around the table. "By the way, where *is* Elmer?"

* * *

Bruno knocked on the door of room 201 in Dormitory 2.

"Come in," came a feeble voice.

Bruno and Boots exchanged a confused look and entered.

The room was normally cluttered with Elmer's experiments, gadgets and inventions, but never before had it appeared so disorganized. The enormous chemistry lab was half on and half off the table. Beakers and flasks lay every which way. One test tube had emptied out onto the floor, where its contents had burned a big hole in the carpet. Elmer's computer workstation was on, but the program appeared to be stuck in an endless loop. All the screen showed was the flashing word *Error*. The printer hammered out this message on reams of continuous paper that had slipped from the desk and were offloading into the fish tank. Frantic tropical fish were darting around in murky, unfiltered water. The many experiment charts on the walls had not been updated in several days.

Elmer sat in the middle of this chaos with his head slumped down on the glass top of his ant farm, looking miserable.

"Elmer!" Bruno exclaimed. "What happened?"

The school genius looked around, but did not seem to notice the junkyard his room had become.

Boots spoke up. "Your room! Your stuff! Your experiments!"

Elmer dismissed this with a wave of his hand. "I can't concentrate on anything. Marylou Beakman hates me."

Bruno's face softened with sympathy. "Aw, Elm, I'm sorry. It was the bird stuff, wasn't it?"

Elmer shrugged miserably. "Who knows? After two rare and special gifts, she never even thanked me. Not a call or a letter. I might as well not exist."

"Wait a minute," said Bruno suspiciously. "You don't

know she hates you. You're just guessing."

Elmer threw his hands up in despair. "What other explanation could there be? She must really despise me to ignore remarkable presents like those. I must be utterly repulsive to her!"

"A million things could have gone wrong," Bruno insisted. "The packages could have got lost in the mail. Or Miss Scrimmage might have delivered them to the wrong room — you know how dizzy she is."

"Or they could have been stolen," Boots jumped in. "Stolen by some frustrated scientist who couldn't get his own rodent skull and bird droppings."

This brought a faint glimmer of hope to Elmer's sad eyes. "Do you really think so?"

"Listen, Elm," said Bruno, "you're not going to get this girl through the mail. You could ship her a whole rain forest by special delivery and it wouldn't help you. The secret of a good relationship is communication."

Elmer nodded in slow understanding. "Fax, right? You think I should fax her."

"Not *that* kind of communication!" managed Boots. Getting through to Elmer was like wading through molasses.

"Look," said Bruno. "The next time we go over to Scrimmage's, you're coming with us. It's time to meet Marylou face to face."

Elmer turned several shades of pale. "But — but it's against the rules — ! Miss Scrimmage has a big dog — ! I wouldn't know what to say!"

"Well, you've got plenty of time to think of something," said Bruno.

"Indubitably!" Elmer began writing furiously in a notebook. He tore off the top sheet and handed it to Bruno.

"*Hello, Marylou,*" Bruno read aloud. "*What is your opinion of the Frummet-Zinkerstein method of transpolar coordinates?*"

"Kind of technical," Boots commented in a strangled voice.

Elmer nodded in reluctant agreement. "Transpolar coordinates can be tricky," he admitted. "Maybe I should start with something simpler, like vector algebra."

"First things first," put in Bruno. "We need to borrow your telescope, okay?"

"Excellent," Elmer approved. He looked around and spotted it stuffed lens-first into the open ant farm. "Help yourself. May I recommend the constellation of Cygnus. On a clear night you can make out a globular cluster between the second and third stars."

"We're not following stars; we're following the movements of Cathy Burton and Diane Grant." He fished the instrument out of the ant farm, brushing away sand and insects. "Hey, Elm, maybe you should get this place cleaned up a little."

"Right," added Boots. "We can help if you want." But Elmer was already back into his notebook, scribbling conversation starters for Marylou.

Chapter 8

traffic jam

A car horn honked. A truck geared down in a roar of machinery. Air brakes whooshed.

Mr. Sturgeon opened one eye and punched his pillow. Where were all these traffic noises coming from? At Macdonald Hall one usually woke to birds singing, crickets chirping and, occasionally, the soothing sound of rain on the roof. The noise from Highway 48 seldom penetrated to the Headmaster's little cottage on the south lawn.

There was a loud blast from an air horn.

Mr. Sturgeon vaulted out of bed, stubbing his sore toe and yelping in pain.

His wife sat up abruptly. "William! What is it?"

He peered through the venetian blinds and gasped. "A traffic jam," he replied in wonder.

"On Route 48?"

"No, on our driveway."

She joined him at the window. Long lines of cars, trucks and vans led off the highway and up the circular drive to the Faculty Building. There the traffic was forced onto the narrow lane that serviced the south lawn. A sharp left looped around the pool building and disappeared from view. But the Sturgeons could make out the tops of transport trucks above the dormitory roofs way over on the north side of the campus. Beyond there, finally, the traffic merged back onto the highway.

Mrs. Sturgeon gawked. "How odd! Why on earth would all the cars come onto our private road?"

The Headmaster's brow clouded. "Unless my eyes deceive me, Mildred, those are detour signs out on the road. Someone has deliberately diverted Route 48 through Macdonald Hall."

She frowned. "But who would want to do that?"

Mr. Sturgeon limped to the closet and shrugged into his red silk bathrobe. "I think we may safely assume that our practical joker has struck again."

"The Phantom!" she exclaimed.

The squealing of brakes under their window made them both jump.

"Please don't use that nickname, Mildred. It glamorizes gross misbehaviour the likes of which I have never seen. When I get my hands on that so-called Phantom, he will *indeed* wish himself a ghost!" He stepped into his slippers.

"But I thought running the school had become a 'no-brainer,'" she put in. "Surely you must know who this person is."

"I have my suspicions," the Headmaster replied, limping out of the room.

"My goodness," she called. "Just after you complained that things were so predictable, here we are in the midst of chaos!"

"I didn't know when I was well-off!" he snapped over his shoulder, and pounded down the stairs.

Stumping along with his cane, he burst out the front door just in time to see Mr. Fudge running toward him. The Dormitory 3 Housemaster was waving his arms in agitation.

"Mr. Sturgeon! There are cars on the campus!"

"Your powers of observation are keen as ever, Fudge," said the Headmaster ironically. He stormed over to his rosebushes where a sign was balanced on the top branches:

DETOUR

A large brown feather was neatly taped to the cardboard. Similar signs stood all along the parade route, guiding bewildered motorists through the maze.

The Headmaster's eyes darted to Route 48, where the notice on a big sawhorse declared:

ROAD CLOSED
USE BYPASS

"I want these signs removed," ordered Mr. Sturgeon, "starting with the ones in the street. Get some of the students to help you. Quickly!"

Mr. Fudge rushed off.

There was a loud hissing sound. Steam began pouring out from under the hood of an elegant Mercedes. It ground to a halt, blocking the road. Horns honked and angry shouts filled the air.

"What's going on up there?"

"Move out!"

"What is this, Times Square?"

A four-by-four was attempting to sneak out of line and get ahead by driving on the lawn. Out of nowhere, the nose of a station wagon swerved right to block its way. A barrage of insults shot back and forth between the two drivers.

"Gentlemen, gentlemen." Mr. Sturgeon rushed into the fray. "I must demand that you watch your language. You are on the grounds of a school."

"Hey, get a load of the guy in the pyjamas!"

Mrs. Sturgeon hurried from her cottage, carrying a bucket of water for the overheated Mercedes.

No sooner had they gotten things going again than Miss Scrimmage's van pulled up, with the Headmistress leaning on the horn.

Mr. Sturgeon turned to his wife. "I was just about to comment that things could not possibly get any worse. How foolish of me."

Miss Scrimmage pulled onto the lawn, knocking over the mailbox. She emerged from behind the wheel, seething with indignation. "What on earth is going on? It has taken me fully twenty minutes to get here from the highway!"

"Why ever are you driving?" exclaimed Mrs. Sturgeon. "You live just across the road!"

"I am returning from Toronto," replied Miss Scrimmage harshly. "From a scientific laboratory."

Mr. Sturgeon was not paying attention. He was busy directing cars around his fallen mailbox, which now jutted right out into the lane.

Miss Scrimmage grabbed the sleeve of his bathrobe and spun him around. "You dare to ignore me, sir?" There was a pop as an eighteen-wheeler drove over the mailbox, squashing it flat as a pancake.

"Your number fifty-seven has struck again!" the Headmistress shrilled. "The same girl who received that repellent little skull was sent *this* package!"

The Headmaster frowned. "Not another voodoo curse?"

"Ha!" Miss Scrimmage fumed. "Voodoo is a mere hobby for such an accomplished terrorist!" She held out the box. "This came with a note claiming that the material in the plastic bag was bird droppings!"

Mr. Sturgeon grimaced. "My goodness! What did you do?"

"I had it analyzed, of course! And you will simply not believe what it is! *Bird droppings!* Of all things!"

The Headmaster took a step backwards. "Well, in that case, will you kindly cease and desist waving it in my face."

Miss Scrimmage choked back tears of rage. "This has been my problem for twenty-five years! I come to you with a legitimate grievance and you mock me!"

Mr. Sturgeon sighed heavily. "I do apologize, Miss Scrimmage. As you can see, I am somewhat distracted at the moment." He indicated the snarl of traffic with a sweep of his arm. "Now, have either of these packages contained, by any chance, a feather?"

"Don't be ridiculous!" snapped the Headmistress. "What do feathers have to do with anything?"

"We have been experiencing some difficulty with a practical joker," Mr. Sturgeon explained patiently. "I thought your incidents might be related."

"Well, this is no joke," Miss Scrimmage retorted crossly. "The poor girl is terrified and so am I. I've instructed my girls that they are to be helpless no longer. We are taking the matter of safety into our own hands. I have brought my shotgun up from the basement, and now sleep with it by my side."

"Your *shotgun?!*" The red flush started at the collar of Mr. Sturgeon's pyjamas and soon turned his face the colour of his bathrobe. "Madam, I have repeatedly told you that you are not fit to be in possession of a firearm! I forbid it!"

In answer, Miss Scrimmage raised her foot and brought it down on the Headmaster's ingrown toenail.

"*Yee-o-o-o-ow!!*"

He began hopping around, cradling his injured foot.

"Would anyone like some tea?" offered Mrs. Sturgeon, ever the peacemaker.

But Miss Scrimmage was already climbing into her van. With a squeal of tires, she backed out into the stream of traffic, narrowly missing a Winnebago. There she sat, looking straight ahead as the line of vehicles inched forward.

The traffic jam was in full swing on the lane that snaked between dormitories 2 and 3. A crowd of pyjama-clad boys was milling around, taking in the rare sight of a big-city rush hour on their quiet campus.

Bruno pulled the feather from the detour sign stuck in the bushes in front of Dormitory 3. "We've got the Phantom this time!" he exclaimed. "We had total surveillance all night, so we'll know which one of our suspects set this up!"

"Well, not *total* surveillance," Boots confessed. "I sort of fell asleep during my shift at the telescope."

"What? For how long?"

Boots hung his head. "Pretty much all of it."

Bruno glared at him. "Aw, Boots — "

Boots looked at him reproachfully. "I'm pretty sure I heard a couple of snores coming from your shift."

Bruno looked startled. "Really? I thought I might have dozed off, but I was hoping I just dreamed it."

Boots sighed. "So Cathy and Diane could have done this and we missed it."

"Maybe it was Mark," said Bruno. "Or Edward. Hey, Sidney!"

Sidney started to cross the road between the two dormitories. But the radio antenna of a passing convertible snagged his arm. In an instant, the antenna was up his sleeve and out the neck of his pyjamas.

"Stop!" croaked Sidney. "Hey — you got me!"

With a noise like popping corn, all the buttons flew off the pyjama top. Sidney twirled once, and suddenly he was shirtless in the cool fall morning. The convertible moved on, flying Sidney's pyjama top from its aerial like a diplomatic flag.

Sidney shuffled over. "Anybody got an extra T-shirt?"

"Never mind that," said Bruno briskly. "Did Mark leave the room last night?"

Sidney shrugged. "How should I know? I was sleeping."

"But you were on surveillance! You weren't supposed to sleep!"

Sidney stared at him. "*Ever?*"

"Forget it," said Boots. "Who was watching Edward?"

"Me," came a deep voice behind them. There stood big Wilbur.

"What's your report?" demanded Bruno.

"Nothing," Wilbur admitted.

"You mean Edward never left his room?" asked Boots.

"I mean I forgot to go on surveillance," said Wilbur, shame-faced. "My shipment from the Decadent Dessert of the Month Club arrived yesterday. It was called 'Death by Chocolate.' Amazing."

"I'd be more worried about death by Walton if I were you!" growled Bruno. "Well, this is just great! The biggest practical joke of all happened, and we don't even have a clue!"

Coach Flynn jogged by, plucking the detour sign out of the bushes. "I guess you find this pretty funny," he growled at them. "It's really hilarious to inconvenience hundreds of people!"

"But it wasn't us!" Boots protested.

"I've heard *that* one before."

Chapter 9

diddly-squat

Cathy slipped into her room, struggled over to her bed and dropped her armload of books.

"Sorry I'm late, Diane. I had trouble getting that cheese-cake to Rex. Miss Smedley's been watching him like a hawk ever since the diet started."

Diane looked up from her homework. "What's with the books?" She squinted at the titles. "*Guerrilla Warfare? Booby Traps for Beginners? Military Fortifications? The Official Special Forces Manual?* Cathy — are we at war?"

"You heard Miss Scrimmage at the assembly," Cathy replied. "She wants us to defend our turf."

"All I heard was that we should keep our eyes open around the school," Diane pointed out.

"And take responsibility for our own security," Cathy finished.

"She's just worried because Marylou got another weird package," Diane argued. "Military fortifications aren't going to keep the post office from delivering another baggie of bird droppings."

"That's the beauty of it," Cathy reasoned. "Miss Scrimmage gave us the green light. We're covered. We can lay booby traps all around the grounds and then say it was her idea."

Diane grimaced. "Maybe. But everyone *except* Miss Scrimmage knows that the only 'intruders' are the guys from Macdonald Hall — and we want them. What's the point of putting up defences?"

Cathy rolled her eyes. "Because it's fun. Don't you get sick of all that baking we do? If I have to spend my day training to be a young lady, I want to blow off a little steam as a commando at night."

Diane sat down on her bed, looking miserable. "Cathy, this is crazy. We can't do it."

"Oh, it's not just *us*," said Cathy airily. "I've recruited tons of girls to help. We meet in the orchard at 2 AM."

* * *

The next day after school, the surveillance team — Bruno, Boots, Pete, Sidney, Larry and Wilbur — met in room 306.

Bruno called the meeting to order. "First of all," he announced, "don't forget to thank Elmer when you see him. It was his idea to hook up the video camera to the telescope so we wouldn't have to stay up all night watching Scrimmage's. It's also his camera and his telescope, so we owe the guy big-time."

"Where *is* Elmer?" asked Larry.

"Well," said Boots, "let's just say he's got a lot on his mind." He knew the school genius was holed up in his room, brainstorming snappy lines for his big meeting with Marylou.

"Now," began Bruno, "I don't have to tell any of you guys about the size fifty-two women's underwear up the flagpole this morning."

Pete snickered, and Bruno fixed him with a withering glare. "It's not funny. There was a feather on those bloomers, so we all know it's a Phantom job." He held up a videocassette. "We were taping all night. If it was Cathy and Diane, we should see them leaving their room."

He popped the tape in the VCR and pushed *Play*. A dark image of the side of Miss Scrimmage's appeared on the screen. The camera was focused on the drainpipe outside Cathy and Diane's window. Bruno hit the *Fast Forward* button and the boys sat back to await developments.

"Great movie," cheered Wilbur. "I nominate the drainpipe for best supporting actor."

"Don't knock it," Larry told him. "It sure beats sitting up all night squinting into a telescope."

Pete yawned. "How long is it going to take to go through the whole thing?"

"Hold it," said Boots suddenly. "Run that back." Bruno rewound for a moment and hit *Play*. For just a few seconds, a shadowy figure darted across the corner of the screen, disappearing behind the building.

"Back up and freeze," ordered Boots.

The picture reversed frame by frame. It was just a silhouette, but the profile shone in the moonlight for a split second.

"Edward!" cried Boots in agony.

Bruno squinted at the screen. "Are you sure?"

Boots held his head. "I grew up with that little jerkface. I'd know him anywhere!"

"He sure likes Scrimmage's," Sidney commented.

Larry frowned. "But the bloomers were on *our* flagpole, not theirs."

"He's up to something," muttered Bruno. "There must be a connection."

"Well, he's not going to see Cathy and Diane," Boots put in. "The only way to their room is straight up the drainpipe."

"Maybe he went to Scrimmage's first to put us off the trail," suggested Wilbur. "Then he doubled back here to put the underwear up the flagpole."

"Gee, too bad we didn't have the telescope focused on the flagpole instead of Scrimmage's," said Sidney.

"Who knew?" shrugged Bruno. "There's no way we can ever predict where the Phantom is going to strike next."

"I say we slap it out of Edward," gritted Boots. "I mean, lean on the kid until he tells us exactly what he *does* over there!"

Bruno shook his head. "Bad idea. If he is the Phantom, we don't want him to know we're onto him. We have to catch him in the act." He hit *Fast Forward* again. "Let's see what else there is."

At first, it looked like a brief flash of white light. Everyone sat forward. Bruno fiddled with the controls and isolated the sudden action.

Pete was the first to recognize it. "Hey, look. It's a guy."

Once again, Bruno advanced frame by frame. The "flash" was caused by someone walking past the telescope. The extreme close-up view of the figure's white T-shirt made the frame seem bright.

"You can't see his face," observed Wilbur, disappointed.

"Maybe it's Edward coming home," suggested Larry.

Boots's keen eyes narrowed. "Hey, what's that on his shirt?"

Bruno sharpened the VCR's focus as best he could. "It's some kind of crest, I think."

Larry picked up a pad and pencil and began to sketch. The crest looked like a greyish egg surrounded by many large and small circles. The whole design was topped off by what seemed to be a crown.

The boys passed the drawing around. All agreed that was pretty much what they saw, too.

"Listen up," said Bruno. "Somebody's got that shirt, and someday he'll wear it again. We want to know why that guy was out the night the underwear went up the pole." He hit *Play* and *Fast Forward* and they continued to scan the tape.

Five minutes went by, then ten. Pete dozed off and began to snore gently. Wilbur tiptoed to the bathroom and back in again. He had missed nothing.

"I wonder what time it is on the tape," mused Sidney.

Bruno flashed the display. "Two hours, fifty-five minutes. We started taping at around eleven, so that makes it almost 2 AM."

"Forget it," grumbled Wilbur. "It's too late. Nothing's going to happen now."

No sooner were the words out of his mouth than a whole

army of figures seemed to explode down the drainpipe.

"Whoa!" cried Bruno. He hacked at the remote control and the tape slowed down to normal speed. It was hard to make out faces, but there were at least thirty girls, most of them weighed down with heavy equipment.

"What are they carrying?" asked Larry.

The girls hit the ground and set to work, but what they were doing was not clear either. The camera had been focused on the drainpipe; the action was all on ground level. Only the bottom corner of the screen displayed vigorous activity. Sticks and shovels shot through the frame; clods of dirt were airborne; blurred faces rushed around; leaves, branches, rope — all passed before the boys' bewildered eyes.

Larry was bug-eyed. "It looks like they're laying the foundation for a fifty-story building!"

There was a mad dash for the telescope. Bruno got there first and focused on the spot where the previous night's activity had taken place.

"There's nothing there," he reported.

"Impossible!" Wilbur replaced him at the eyepiece. "From the action on that tape, we could be across from the SkyDome by now."

"Maybe they're digging a tunnel," said Sidney. He got a pillow across the back of the head for his suggestion.

"Well, I'm totally confused," said Boots, aggravated. "I mean, have we learned anything here?"

"Let's make a list," Bruno decided.

1. Edward was out, but in the wrong place to put the bloomers up the flagpole. That doesn't mean he didn't do it before or after appearing on the video.

2. Somebody wearing a white T-shirt with a crest on it was out on the campus. Insignia: unknown. Identity: unknown. Mission: unknown.

3. A large number of girls were involved in a major operation at Scrimmage's. However, there is no sign of what they built and no proof that any of this was Phantom-related.

4. Cathy and Diane may or may not have had the chance to sneak over to Macdonald Hall and put the underwear up the flagpole.

"In other words," groaned Wilbur, "we know diddly-squat."

Sidney was examining the list. "I'm getting a headache."

Pete's eyelids fluttered and he yawned himself awake. His gaze fell on the TV and VCR. "Oh, a movie. What did I miss?"

"The most baffling mystery in the history of the world!" growled Bruno. "But it's not over yet!"

Chapter 10

counting shirts

Mr. Sturgeon's ingrown toenail suffered greatly from being stomped on by Miss Scrimmage. The entire toe turned purple and grew even more swollen. Every step was misery.

His limp worsened, along with his mood. Finally, at the urging of his wife, the Headmaster called the doctor.

"Well," said Dr. Haupt, "the accident really aggravated your condition."

"It was no accident," said Mr. Sturgeon darkly. "I was attacked by a crazy person."

The young doctor looked shocked. "Really? Who?"

"Oh, the Headmistress of the finishing school across the road."

Dr. Haupt raised an eyebrow. "If this is the work of a Headmistress, I'd hate to see what a hired assassin could do." He packed up his medical bag. "I can prescribe a stronger painkiller to help you get a good night's rest."

The Headmaster shook his head. "I'm out like a corpse from the pills I already have. I sleep so heavily my wife has been taking my pulse to make sure I'm still alive."

The doctor shrugged. "I'm sorry, but my prognosis remains the same." He opened the office door. "You need the operation. Nothing else is going to do any good."

* * *

" . . . that's exactly what the doctor said!" Larry told Bruno and Boots as he handed over photocopies of his sketch of the crest. "I was right there by the Xerox machine making these and I heard every word."

Classes were over for the day and the boys were heading in the direction of the dormitories.

"That doesn't sound good," said Bruno. "The Fish definitely needs an operation."

"The doctor said nothing else would help," Larry added breathlessly.

"But what *kind* of operation?" Boots asked.

"What difference does it make?" said Bruno. "It's an operation and that's serious." He shuddered. "Poor guy. On top of it all, he's got the Phantom to worry about."

"The Fish isn't worrying too much about the Phantom," Boots said feelingly. "He thinks it's us. So does half the school."

"He *suspects* it's you," Larry corrected. "Don't worry. The Fish would never suspend a guy unless he was sure."

Bruno slapped his photocopy. "Well, at least now we can

go to Edward's room. If he's got a shirt with this crest on it, he's got a lot to answer for!"

* * *

Edward O'Neal opened the door of room 105 in Dormitory 1 and peered into the hall at Bruno and Boots.

"Well, what do you know?" he announced sarcastically. "It's the Over-the-Hill gang."

Bruno and Boots brushed past him into the room.

"I got a letter from Mom today," said Boots. "She wants me to come in here and make sure you've got enough shirts."

Edward's eyes narrowed. "That is such a bad lie, it's pathetic."

Boots stuck out his jaw. "I'm counting your shirts."

"Show me the letter," said Edward defiantly.

"You want to see the letter? Here's the letter!" Like lightning, Boots whirled his brother around and clamped him tightly in a hammerlock. "Okay, Bruno," he called over the yelling. "Start counting!"

Bruno pulled the photocopy out of his pocket and began to rifle through the closet, looking for a white T-shirt with that particular crest.

The door opened and Edward's roommate, a small, slight boy, entered. He gasped with fright. "Wh–what's going on?"

"We're counting shirts," said Boots through clenched teeth.

"Eight — nine — ten — " called Bruno from the closet. "And now the drawers — eleven — twelve — "

"Call the Housemaster!" Edward ordered. "I'm being mugged!"

"I wouldn't do that," Boots cautioned mildly. "Not unless you want us to count your shirts next."

"Nothing," reported Bruno. "And nothing in the laundry bag, either."

Boots released his brother. "Okay, kid, you've got enough shirts. I'll tell Mom."

Edward bit back his rage. "You guys aren't just old; you're *senile!*"

"It was a pleasure doing business with you," Bruno grinned as the two sauntered out of the room. He fixed Boots with a look of deep satisfaction. "It's our one advantage over your stupid brother. We're bigger than he is."

Boots grimaced. "He'll probably take up karate and kill us both."

An enormous crash came from the far end of the hall. Dormitory 1 seemed to jar beneath their feet.

"What was that?" asked Boots.

Bruno laughed. "It might have been an atomic bomb, but my guess is it was a dresser tipping over on Sidney."

Boots looked blank. "How could you know that?"

"Elementary, my dear Melvin. Mark is another suspect. And his shirts need 'counting' too."

* * *

Cathy had picked up music videos on her ten-inch TV. She was rampaging around the room, playing "air guitar" along with the band, complete with cartwheels and high kicks.

Diane was not joining in the fun. "Cut it out, Cathy. You're going to put yourself through a wall."

Cathy launched into a series of flying power chords. A small vase toppled from her dresser and smashed on the floor.

Diane shut off the TV. "Control yourself!" she demanded, picking up the pieces of broken porcelain.

"Since when did you turn into Miss Scrimmage?" Cathy laughed. She sat down on her bed, but continued to bounce up and down to the music that was no longer there.

"I'm not Miss Scrimmage," Diane defended herself. "I'm just not ballistic like you."

"You're worse than Miss Scrimmage," Cathy accused. "Take last night. We did a totally cool thing and you whined and complained through the whole deal."

"We broke at least fifty rules," Diane argued, "and probably twenty laws. And for what? Some gag to protect ourselves from nothing."

"Totally untrue," Cathy retorted. "Look at poor Marylou. She's walking around with a voodoo curse on her head!"

"Even *she* doesn't believe that!" snapped Diane.

"And Rex," Cathy persisted. "He's been deliberately de-Tyrannosaurus-ed. It could be part of the voodoo curse — "

"That was *us!*" Diane exploded.

"Or a separate curse altogether! Or an international conspiracy of dog-overfeeders!"

"Give me a break," groaned Diane.

"Look," said Cathy. "Miss Scrimmage was worried about security." She spread her arms wide. "We're a fortress now. The marines couldn't land here without sustaining heavy losses!"

"That's the problem," said Diane. "What if Miss Scrimmage takes an evening stroll? What if the gardener blunders a little off course? What if poor Rex gets caught in all that stuff? Now that we've fattened him up, he's the sweetest thing on four pudgy legs. The girls'll kill us if anything happens to him!"

"No biggie," said Cathy. "If Rex disappears, we'll know where to look."

"Okay — " Diane played her trump card, "what if Bruno and Boots try to come over? Do you want *them* to sustain heavy losses like the marines?"

"I've already thought of that," said Cathy smugly. From her desk drawer, she pulled out a piece of paper. "We did mapmaking in geography today. Mine is the apple orchard and the trees out front, with all our defences and booby traps marked in red. I got an A, but only because I told Miss Riggens it was Greenland."

Diane made a face. "That map is going to do Bruno and Boots a fat lot of good in your desk drawer."

Cathy blinked. "Didn't I mention it? We're taking it over there — in about ten minutes."

* * *

It was just after midnight when Cathy and Diane stole across the highway onto the Macdonald Hall property. It was a routine trip for the girls. They had been to visit Bruno and Boots countless times over the years. Even so, Diane still felt the butterflies in her stomach as they left the open lawn and zeroed in on Dormitory 3.

Cathy rapped smartly on the window of room 306. "I can't believe it's three weeks into school and the only times we've seen Bruno and Boots, they've been running away from Miss Scrimmage."

"Not so loud," hissed Diane. "You'll wake up the Housemaster."

Cathy laughed. "Mr. Fudge? He can't hear anything over

the sound of his own snoring." She knocked again. "Where are those guys?" She pressed her face up to the glass. "I don't see anybody in there."

Diane frowned. "It's after midnight. Where could they be?" Suddenly, she went white to the ears. "Oh, no! You don't think we missed them in the dark and they're on their way over to see us?"

Cathy was silent for a while. "Uh-oh," she said finally. From her pocket she produced the folded map. "I'll bet they could make pretty good use of *this* along about now."

Chapter 11

the romance of swamp germs

"Hey, Elmer, how come you're bringing your science notes to Scrimmage's?"

It was just after midnight and Bruno, Boots, Larry, Wilbur, Pete, Sidney and Elmer were stealing across the Macdonald Hall campus.

Elmer spied the small card in Pete's hand. "They aren't notes!" he hissed. "They're conversation starters for when I meet Marylou Beakman!"

Pete was confused. "But it's about swamp germs."

Elmer's flushed, red face seemed to glow in the darkness as he glared at the boys one by one. "I am terrified of what will happen if I am caught violating the curfew! I am petrified of Miss Scrimmage's school because every time I go there something awful happens! I am bowed down with raw fear at the thought of meeting Marylou Beakman tonight! Give me that!" He snatched the card out of Pete's hand. "My romantic life is none of your business!"

"I never knew swamp germs were romantic," put in Sidney.

"If you comedians are through making stupid jokes," said Bruno, "I can remind you we've got a job to do. We have to find out what the girls were doing last night on the videotape. Let's go."

They soldiered on, with Sidney bringing up the rear. In single file, the seven boys crossed the highway and moved silently over the fence.

Bruno dropped to the grass. "Okay, stick together and stay close to the trees," he whispered. "Who's got the dog biscuits in case Rex shows up?"

Pete held up a bag. "Right here. We didn't have dog biscuits so I had to bring bagel chips."

"Hey, toss me a couple of those," said Wilbur. "I'm getting kind of hungry."

Elmer spoke up, his voice shaking. "You said Rex wasn't a worry because he was too fat and lazy."

"Oh, he's too fat to *attack*," explained Boots. "But if he starts barking, we'll have Miss Scrimmage on our necks."

Bruno led the group into the trees. He counted heads and came up short. "Hey, wait a second. There's supposed to be seven of us. Who's missing?" The boys took stock of each other.

"Oh, no!" Boots exclaimed. "Where's Sidney?"

"Probably where he always is," said Wilbur in disgust. "Flat on his face somewhere."

"All right," sighed Bruno. "Let's find him before the buzzards do."

They spread out and began feeling through the grass for Sidney's form. One by one, they checked in with Bruno.

"Nothing," said Larry.

"No luck," added Boots.

"He seems to have vanished," confirmed Elmer.

"He's capital-G gone," Wilbur moaned.

Bruno listened for Pete's report. It did not come. "Aw, no, not another one! What's going on here?"

The boys couldn't believe their eyes. Now Pete was missing too!

"This is really weird," breathed Boots. "It's like there's a bear out there, eating us one at a time!"

"That's horrible!" quavered Elmer.

"You're telling me," Wilbur said morosely. "Pete was carrying the bagel chips."

Larry pulled his sweater tighter around him. "What are we going to do?" He took a shaky step backward and, before the boys' astonished eyes, he vanished.

"Whoa!" cried Bruno, heedless of the need to keep quiet. "Did anybody else see that?"

"He just — disappeared — " Boots barely whispered.

"There is no scientific explanation for what we have just witnessed," was Elmer's analysis. "It is a paranormal phenomenon."

Then they heard it — a faint voice.

"Help! . . . "

"That's Larry!" exclaimed Bruno.

They ran to the spot where the office messenger had just been standing.

"Larry!" called Boots. "Where are you?"

"Down here!" echoed the reply.

"Down?" repeated Bruno. *"Where?"*

"In a hole!" came Larry's answer. "It's really deep, too!"

Once again, the group dropped to their hands and knees and began feeling through the leaves and grass.

Boots came upon the pit first. "Over here!" he hissed.

The hole was about a metre across, but half of the opening was still covered with leaves resting on a grill of small branches. The other half yawned open. They could just make out Larry's white face looking up at them from below the surface.

"Man," said Bruno, "you fell down so fast, it looked like you just winked off the face of the earth!"

"Sure scared me," added Boots. "We've been coming here for years. Since when is there a giant crater at Scrimmage's?"

Elmer regarded the sticks and leaves. "Most curious," he began thoughtfully. "A deep hole camouflaged by ground cover is most commonly used in jungle warfare."

Bruno snapped his fingers. "Those crazy girls laid booby traps all around the school! That's what they were doing on the video last night — digging holes for us to fall into!"

Wilbur was mystified. "Why would they want to do that?"

Bruno frowned. "Maybe Cathy and Diane are the Phantom and this is their latest joke."

Boots shrugged helplessly. "Cathy could pull something like this just to pass the time, Phantom or no! She's done worse with less reason!"

"Larry," ordered Bruno, "dig around down there and see if you can find a feather."

Larry spat out mud and brushed some leaves from his hair. "Aren't we forgetting something?" he said sarcastically. "How about pulling me out of here?"

Bruno reached an arm down into the hole.

"Halt!"

"It's Miss Scrimmage!" hissed Boots.

Bruno, Boots, Elmer and Wilbur took off for the cover of the apple orchard.

"Hey, what about me?" Larry wailed.

"Keep a low profile!" Bruno advised on the run.

Larry clawed the earthen walls. "I've got a *choice?*"

"Stop, intruders!" Miss Scrimmage's voice rang out.

The boys cut around the side of the school. One of Wilbur's heavy footfalls came down on a small wire which was hooked up to the top of a tree. From a high branch, a gigantic net was released. It flopped down on the big boy, tripping him up. He thrashed on the ground, helplessly entangled.

"Did you see that?" panted Boots. "This place is a death trap!"

As they ran around the back of the school, Elmer's ankle snapped a string that was covered by a pile of leaves. From the top of a tall birch, a basketball on the end of a rope was airborne. It fell in a lazy arc, missing Elmer's elbow by a hair. Then, the ball swung back, the rope wrapping around Elmer's fleeing form. It whirled around him like an orbiting moon. By the time the ball came up under his chin, he was hog-tied, his arms fastened to his sides by coils of rope.

"Oh, man!" groaned Bruno, accelerating. "Oh, man! Oh, *man!*"

Suddenly, Boots's flailing arm struck a low branch. He spun around and hit the ground in a hail of apples. Bruno put on the brakes and bent over his roommate. "Are you okay — ?"

"*Aha!* Intruders, *freeze!*"

From behind a row of dwarf trees stepped Miss Scrimmage, her eyes blazing in the night. Bruno and Boots gasped in terror. The Headmistress was carrying her shotgun.

* * *

"Wasn't that a delightful opera, dear?" asked Mrs. Sturgeon as she and her husband drove north on Highway 48 on their way back to Macdonald Hall.

Mr. Sturgeon yawned and flashed his lights at an oncoming truck. "I suppose it was all right. But it's a long way to drive and it's awfully late. Why do they always hold these things in Toronto?"

His wife laughed. "Because they tried staging them in some farmer's barn, but the scenery wouldn't fit in the hayloft. You *love* the opera, William. Why are you being so cranky?"

"It's my medical condition, Mildred. Just as I'm about to immerse myself in Verdi, a twinge of pain shoots up from my toe and lands me back in the discomfort that has become my life."

His wife rolled her eyes. "I'm afraid I have no more sympathy for you, William. You heard the doctor. It's such a small operation — "

All at once, two figures ran out into the road in front of them. Mr. Sturgeon slammed on the brakes and the car screeched to a halt. For a moment, the headlights illuminated Cathy Burton and Diane Grant scrambling back across the highway to their own school.

He rolled down the window and called out, "Miss Burton — "

Through the night came the unmistakable scream of Miss Scrimmage: "*Aha!* Intruders *freeze!*"

It meant only one thing: some of his boys had been caught on Miss Scrimmage's property. He was transported back to the day of the traffic jam. Miss Scrimmage's words echoed through his head:

" . . . I'm bringing my shotgun up from the basement . . . "

"Good Lord!" He leaped from the car, forgetting his cane and the fact that his toe was on fire with pain.

"William, what on earth — ?"

But her husband was in full flight, hobbling at top speed, intent on rescuing his students.

He caught up with Cathy and Diane just inside the orchard.

"Sir!" quavered Diane. "We didn't do anything! Honest!"

"Stand aside!" Mr. Sturgeon ordered. "Your Headmistress has lost control once again!"

"But the whole orchard is booby-trapped!" Diane blurted.

The Headmaster gawked. *"What? Why?"*

"It seemed like a good idea at the time," Cathy admitted. "But right now a few of your guys are probably caught down holes and stuff. You know how it is."

"I most certainly do not!" Mr. Sturgeon snapped.

"Well, follow us," Cathy instructed. "We've got all the traps memorized. You'll be safe."

The girls picked their way through the orchard, leading

the Headmaster of Macdonald Hall. Not far from the edge of the trees, Cathy and Diane halted.

"Uh-oh — " Cathy began.

Mr. Sturgeon pushed past them and gaped in horror. Walton and O'Neal stood quavering against a gnarled old apple tree. Miss Scrimmage advanced upon them, her shotgun at the ready in her hands.

Mr. Sturgeon ran out in front of Bruno and Boots. "Put down that weapon, Miss Scrimmage," he said quietly.

"They're trespassing!" she shrilled.

Mr. Sturgeon was under tight control. "It is a minor crime when compared with the menace to life and limb represented by you. How dare you make accusations while you hold a gun on children, in the midst of an orchard that is bristling with hazardous booby traps?"

"Booby traps?" Miss Scrimmage was infuriated. "Sir, you are deranged! This is a school for young ladies! There are no booby traps here!"

She took a menacing step forward.

"Miss Scrimmage!" cried Cathy. *"No!"*

The Headmistress's foot came down in some leaves. At the bottom of the pile, her heel knocked away a small peg. A loop of rope closed on her ankle. There was a singing sound as a bent-over tree snapped upright, pulling with it the snare around Miss Scrimmage's leg. Up went the tree, the rope and the Headmistress. She hung there by one ankle, upended, waving her arms and shrieking.

It seemed as though the world stood still, presenting this frozen diorama: Bruno and Boots huddled under the trees; Cathy and Diane pointing in horror; Mr. Sturgeon staring in slack-jawed wonder; and Miss Scrimmage, still clutching her shotgun, swinging upside down like a pendulum.

Cathy was the first to find her voice. "Well, what do you know?" she said in awe. "The book was right. It *does* work!"

* * *

Tyrannosaurus Rex was having a lazy evening. He had polished off a truly astonishing amount of rice pudding, snuck out to him one bowl at a time by his admirers — the girls. He knew perfect contentment. His old attack-dog job could never compare with the comfortable life of a pampered pet.

It was time for a nap — only, who could sleep with all that commotion coming from the orchard?

He trotted around the back of the school. There he came upon Elmer Drimsdale, still trussed up like a turkey, with the basketball in his lap.

Elmer was petrified. "Aaagh! Don't eat me! *Help!*"

Rex wagged his tail. Obviously, this friendly person wanted to play. He reached out a big sloppy tongue and licked Elmer from chin to hairline.

"Aaagh!" In terror, Elmer rolled away onto his back.

And, looking straight up, he saw it. The lights were on in a single second-floor room. There, framed by the window, was the face of Marylou Beakman. He felt a great surge of emotion. She looked twenty times more ravishing than he remembered from the Summer Science Fair. He watched as she opened the window and leaned out. He half expected her to say, *"Elmer, Elmer, wherefore art thou, Elmer?"*

But this blissful vision was shattered as he watched a

visitor climb out of her window onto the TV antenna mast. Elmer couldn't make out the person's face as the figure descended to the ground. But one thing was certain — the visitor was male.

All the fears and shocks and disasters of tonight were replaced by a much deeper tragedy.

Marylou Beakman already had a boyfriend!

Chapter 12

living on the edge

When Mr. Sturgeon limped home for lunch on Saturday, he found his wife staked out on the porch of their small cottage.

"Well?" she asked anxiously.

The Headmaster smiled serenely. "I had a brisk and busy morning, thank you. What's for lunch?"

"That's not what I mean," said Mrs. Sturgeon, annoyed. "I want you to tell me that you weren't too hard on those poor boys."

The Headmaster breezed past her, dropped his cane in the umbrella stand and settled himself at the kitchen table. "I dispensed punishment, which, as you will recall, is my job."

"But don't you think the boys have suffered enough?" she pleaded. "They were trapped in holes, tangled in nets, tied up like criminals. They were filthy and shivering with cold and fear. Poor Elmer Drimsdale was almost in tears."

"If they had stayed in their beds," said her husband implacably, "none of that suffering would have taken place. Our rule book does not state, 'Lights-out is at ten; you might consider going to sleep if you have absolutely nothing better to do.'"

His wife frowned. "Well, I certainly hope you're not picking on the boys because you can't seem to catch up with this Phantom of yours."

"The Phantom is another matter entirely. I will catch him soon enough. And when I do, you will know the true meaning of punishment."

"You're awful." Mrs. Sturgeon placed a steaming bowl of soup in front of him. "And you were certainly awful to poor Miss Scrimmage last night. How could you leave her in the tree for almost an hour?"

The Headmaster set his jaw. "My students were still in booby traps set out by her barbarians. Until our boys were safe, it made no difference to me if she were hanging by the *neck!*"

"What on earth might have possessed the girls to do it?"

Mr. Sturgeon shrugged. "Perhaps the traps were meant for that horrible dog. Or maybe they thought it might protect them from their voodoo curse. I have given up trying to understand those so-called young ladies from across the road. They are all as mentally stable as their Headmistress."

"Well, I've just spoken with her," said Mrs. Sturgeon

coldly. "She says that she has been phoning your office and that you will not respond to her calls."

"That is untrue," the Headmaster defended himself. "I dispatched a memo by third-class mail asking if I had the honour of addressing the right-side-up Miss Scrimmage or the upside-down Miss Scrimmage."

A giggle escaped Mrs. Sturgeon, but her expression remained severe. "I'd like to see you display this type of humour where your sore toe is concerned."

A boyish grin broke through the Headmaster's stern exterior. "Mildred, the sight of Miss Scrimmage whipping through the air in that booby trap was the most stupendous thing I have ever witnessed. If my sore toe were to spread up my leg, through my torso and into my brain and kill me, I would die a happy man for having seen it!"

* * *

Boots O'Neal stepped out of the back entrance of the Faculty Building carrying an armload of chalk erasers. He picked up two and began to pound them until his whole body was enveloped in a cloud of yellow dust. He backed away, snorting and sneezing.

"*Gesundheit,*" called Sidney, who was picking up litter with a pointed stick. "Ow!" he added, missing a gum wrapper and jamming the sharp spike into his foot.

"Hey," called Boots, "how about we swap? I'll go on garbage and you guys can do the erasers."

"In your dreams," came a low grumble from Wilbur, who was sweeping leaves from the steps. "I have to preserve my nose. Taste is ninety percent smell, you know."

"Ah, there you are." Edward O'Neal breezed up to his brother, waving a piece of paper. "I just got a letter from

Mom. She's pretty worried about you being in trouble all the time."

Boots stiffened. "She doesn't know anything about this."

"She says," Edward pretended to read, "*Melvin has gone astray* — "

"That's not a real letter!" Boots exploded. "That's the flier from Schmidt's Fertilizers!"

Edward smiled sweetly. "I still think it's pretty weird that I'm the one Mom said to watch, and you're the one who's pounding erasers."

"Hey, you're not off the hook yet!" Boots challenged. "What's your math grade? And what are you doing over at Scrimmage's? And how would you like a knuckle sandwich?"

"Math is cruising along, no problem," Edward replied serenely. "I've got everything under control — which is a lot more than I can say for you." He turned on his heel and strolled away. Boots bounced a chalk eraser off his back.

"I guess you guys aren't very close," commented Wilbur dryly.

"Sure we are," said Boots. "Close to killing each other."

Bruno stepped out of the Faculty Building, struggling under the weight of a large bucket. "That's it," he gasped. "All the blackboards are washed. I've got a broken back, but, hey, it's a small price to pay." With a groan of effort, he dumped out the bucket in the nearest clump of bushes. "Who's that guy?"

A slim figure in a grey sweatsuit was chugging toward them at a slow but relentless pace. There was something very non-athletic about the jogger. He held his neck stiffly, and his arms didn't move at all. His thick glasses were completely steamed up by his panting breath. Perspiration coated his crew cut, giving his head the look of a prickly glazed donut.

Boots made the identification first. *"Elmer?"*

Elmer stopped. He lifted up his fogged glasses and peered at them, owl eyed. "Oh, hello."

"Elm," said Bruno, "what are you doing?"

"I am becoming physically fit," replied Elmer with determination. "Marylou Beakman's boyfriend climbed an entire antenna tower as easily as one factors a polynomial. I must be ready to compete."

"But you're supposed to be on punishment with us," Boots pointed out. "Quick, grab a rake before the Fish sees you!"

Elmer dismissed this with a snort. "If Mr. Sturgeon wants the leaves raked — he's got arms."

The boys gaped. Timid little Elmer usually lived in terror of anything that might land him in trouble.

Bruno found his voice first. "Elmer, are you okay? This could land you up to your nostrils in the soup!"

Elmer shrugged. "All my life I've worked hard and obeyed every rule, and what has it gotten me? Rejected. Well, this is the new Elmer."

"The new Elmer is going to get expelled," warned Boots.

"The new Elmer lives on the edge," the school genius insisted. "I'm taking kick-boxing lessons, and I'm saving up for a motorcycle. I've changed my career ambition from paleobotanist to lion tamer, and I start bungee jumping as soon as my mother returns the permission form. And in spite of all warnings, I have sent in my application to join the Music-by-Mai...

"No!" chorused the boys.

"Look, Elm," said Bruno, "I know you'..
Marylou What's-her-face is with this o..
you've got to pull yourself together."

But Elmer had started to jog in place, sh...
with an imaginary opponent.

"Hey, Elmer," put in Boots, "your thumb goes *outside*
your fist."

Elmer made the adjustment and continued his "bout."
"Well, if you wish to be sheep and follow the rules, that's
your decision. Some of us, however, have lives." And he
jogged off.

"He's flipped out again," Boots observed sadly.

Larry and Pete crept by, lugging enormous green
garbage bags filled with leaves.

"Hey, wasn't that Elmer out jogging?" asked Pete. "I
thought he was on leaf-raking with us."

"If anybody asks, Elmer was here all day," Bruno
announced. "We've got to cover for him during his temporary insanity."

"You mean *we* have to rake *his* leaves?" complained Larry.

Wilbur made a face. "The last time I took your advice,
Bruno, I spent two hours in Scrimmage's apple orchard
tangled up like a total idiot."

"That was part of our Phantom investigation," Bruno
defended himself.

"And after all we've been through," Larry added sarcastically, "we sure know all there is to know about the
Phantom."

"We know that Cathy and Diane were coming back from

they ran into the Fish," replied Bruno.
...ts to them."

...re's just one problem," said Sidney. "There was no
practical joke today."

"Unless what we fell in last night was the joke," put in
Pete.

"I almost hope they *are* the Phantom," Boots said
slowly. "At least that sort of explains the booby traps.
Otherwise, I'm pretty sure we have to kill them for what
they put us through."

"There's another suspect we haven't even considered,"
Larry said thoughtfully. "Marylou Beakman's boyfriend.
Elmer couldn't identify him, none of us saw him and he
was smart enough not to blunder into any of those booby
traps."

Wilbur groaned. "You know, if we're going to get anywhere in all this, the suspect list is supposed to get
smaller, not bigger."

"It will," Bruno promised. "Come on, let's finish up so
we can plan the next step in our investigation."

* * *

When Cathy and Diane were called in to see Miss
Scrimmage, it was not to her office, but upstairs to her
private quarters. The Headmistress had taken to her bed
and lay with a cold cloth on her head and a hot water bottle at her feet. It was from this position that she con-
fronted the architects of the orchard booby traps.

"Oh, Miss Scrimmage!" Cathy exclaimed, all sympathy
and remorse. "We're so, so sorry! Never in a million years
did we dream that you would be the one to get caught in
our best booby trap!"

Just talking about it brought all the horrible events of last night back to Miss Scrimmage. "But why were there *any* booby traps at all?" she wailed.

Cathy looked confused. "*You* told us, Miss Scrimmage."

The Headmistress sat bolt upright, sending the cold cloth and the hot water bottle flying. "*I* told you to turn our school into a war zone?"

Cathy nodded solemnly. "You said we should all take the initiative for our own security."

"I meant we should all try to be a little more watchful!" Miss Scrimmage was losing control. "No one said anything about booby traps!"

Cathy elbowed Diane in the ribs. In perfect unison, both girls burst into tears.

"We thought it would be a happy surprise for you," Diane blubbered. "We worked so hard to make you proud of us. We had no idea that you were going to get *creamed!*"

The Headmistress stared at them in shock.

"It wouldn't have been so bad if it had been one of the holes!" Cathy bawled. "Or even the net! But the tree! Oh, the tree! You really got hung out to dry! How will we ever live with ourselves?"

"Oh, please, girls, don't cry!" begged Miss Scrimmage in genuine distress. "It — it wasn't so bad — "

"Yes, it was! It was *worse!*" Cathy sobbed.

"Nonsense, Catherine. Hanging by the ankle is excellent for the circulation. And Mr. Sturgeon did cut me down — eventually."

"So you forgive us?" sniffled Diane.

"Forgive you?" Miss Scrimmage bounded out of bed and began straightening her hair in the mirror. "I'm *grateful* to you for the initiative you've shown. Only," she turned to look at them, "please try not to show *quite* so much initiative next time."

"Yes, Miss Scrimmage," chorused the girls.

"You have nothing to blame yourselves for," the Headmistress went on. "I never should have placed our security upon your slender shoulders. You know, hanging upside down allows one to think with remarkable clarity. I now realize that these matters must be left to the professionals."

Cathy turned pale. "Professionals?" she repeated.

The Headmistress smiled, her eyes alight with determination. "Our school has just placed an order for the finest and most up-to-date electronic security system in the world — the SectorWatch Fortress Ultra-Deluxe with the patented Banshee II alarm siren."

Chapter 13

the smoking gun

Boots O'Neal rolled over and opened his eyes, shivering. The window was wide open, letting in a sharp, cold breeze. He glanced over to Bruno's bed. It was empty. He looked around the room and discovered that he was alone.

He jumped out of bed and struggled into a pair of jeans and a sweater. Making straight for the window, he silently eased himself over the sill. He jumped to the ground and paused, surveying the deserted campus. Bruno was his best friend, but he could be wildly unpredictable. Boots wondered where he should look first.

Keeping close to the cover of the bushes, he crept around the corner of the building. There he could make out the other two dormitories. No lights were on; all seemed quiet.

He and Bruno had once had a secret whistle to call to each other. But that had been back during their first year at Macdonald Hall. Did he even remember what the whistle was? Would Bruno recognize it if he heard it?

"Hey!"

A dark figure dropped from the roof, bowling Boots over and knocking the wind out of him. The two rolled on the ground, wrestling. Boots got a hand in his attacker's face and pushed hard to try to break free. But the assailant was too strong. Boots felt himself being rolled over onto his stomach. Two knees pressed into the small of his back. His face in the mud, his struggles useless, Boots wondered if he had been jumped by the Phantom himself.

"You're busted, pal!"

Wait a minute! That voice sounded familiar. He was hauled to his feet and came face to face with —

"Bruno!"

"Boots, what are you doing here? I thought you were the Phantom!"

"I was looking for you!" Boots hissed, wiping a smear of mud from his face. "Thanks for the broken back!"

"Well, this is just great!" complained Bruno. "You get all my hopes up and I think I've caught the Phantom and it turns out to be just dumb old you."

Boots's eyes blazed. "I thought we agreed that it was impossible to stake out the whole campus for the Phantom."

"I know," Bruno admitted sheepishly. "But I couldn't sleep. I can't get it out of my head that the Phantom hasn't done anything in two whole days. He's *bound* to be up to something tonight."

"And did you see anything — besides me?"

Bruno shook his head glumly. "Not so much as a firefly. Three cars on the highway. Other than that, nothing. It's even quiet at Scrimmage's."

Boots put a sympathetic arm around his roommate's shoulder. "You said it yourself — there's too much campus to watch, too many suspects and too many hours in a night. If we couldn't do it with a whole bunch of guys, how are you supposed to manage it all by yourself? Face it; if you saw anything, it would be by pure fluke."

And then the shadows moved.

Bruno and Boots both saw it at the same time. On the front lawn of the school, behind the old War of 1812 cannon, a lone figure emerged from the thicket.

"Let's go!" exclaimed Bruno. He set off at a gallop, Boots hot on his heels. The two boys descended like avenging angels on the front lawn of the school. They were about halfway to the cannon when the black-clad figure saw them coming. The silhouette bolted, running away from the lights of the Faculty Building and melting into the surrounding darkness.

"After him!" shouted Bruno. "Don't let him get away!"

Boots turned on the jets. He shot past Bruno and disappeared into the gloom after the fleeing figure. When Bruno caught up with him a few seconds later, Boots was doubled over, gasping.

"We lost him!" Boots panted.

Bruno squinted into the darkness. "He could have gone in any one of fifteen directions. We'll never find him now."

"But what was he doing at the cannon?" Boots wheezed.

The boys jogged back to the thicket at the centre of the lawn. They stopped and stared.

There was just enough light from inside the Faculty Building to make out the antique cannon pointing stalwartly south. Sticking out of the muzzle, like a human cannonball, were the head, arms and torso of a man.

Bruno gasped. "What the — ?"

Cautiously, they moved closer. The human cannonball was a department store mannequin, stuffed feet-first down the barrel of the cannon. Its arms were flung wide. A painted smile grinned out from under a set of plastic joke glasses with eyebrows, mustache, and nose attached. The head sported a soft fedora. Stuck in the hatband was a long, brown feather.

Bruno snatched up the feather, gnashing his teeth. "That was the Phantom — the *real* Phantom! We had him! And we lost him!"

"Hold it right there!"

Twin flashlight beams cut through the gloom, momentarily blinding Bruno and Boots.

Coach Flynn stepped forward, with Mr. Fudge at his side.

"Walton," the gym teacher said grimly. "And O'Neal. I knew it."

"Coach — " said Bruno urgently. "We saw the Phantom! We chased him and — "

"I saw the Phantom, too," interrupted Coach Flynn. "I'm looking at him right now."

"But — but — but it's not us!" stammered Boots.

"Oh, really?" said Mr. Fudge sarcastically.

Bruno and Boots both realized at the same time that the Housemaster was looking at the brown feather still clutched in Bruno's right hand.

A camera flash went off in their faces. All at once, Mark

Davies was upon them, thrusting a microphone in their faces. "Would you care to make a statement for the *Student Times?*"

"Cut it out, Mark!" cried Bruno. "This isn't funny!"

The mike was shifted to the two teachers. "How does it feel to finger the notorious Phantom?"

"Enough!" snapped the coach. "Let's all get some sleep." He turned to Bruno and Boots. "Walton, O'Neal, no classes for you tomorrow morning. You're confined to your room until Mr. Sturgeon decides what to do with you."

* * *

PHANTOM CAPTURED blazoned the *Macdonald Hall Student Times.* The entire first page of this special edition was taken up with the photograph of Bruno and Boots at the cannon, looking startled and guilty.

by Mark Davies, Student Times Reporter

In the shadow of the cannon late last night, a drama unfolded that put an end to the greatest mystery that has ever gripped our school. As this reporter looked on, Mr. Flynn and Mr. Fudge were able to apprehend the serial practical joker known as the Phantom.

The Phantom, who has been baffling teachers and students alike, turns out to be not one person, but two. Bruno Walton and Melvin "Boots" O'Neal (pictured above) were captured in the act of stuffing a mannequin into the cannon. The brown feather held by one of the suspects is known to be the Phantom's trademark. Both are confined to their room awaiting a decision from Mr. Sturgeon.

Further details, p. 3

Scrimmage's to install new security system in wake of booby trap fiasco, p. 4

* * *

Boots O'Neal was in a daze. "He called me Melvin," he said, staring straight ahead. "I hate that name."

Bruno threw down the paper. "I'll kill him!" he seethed. "I'll hunt him down like a dog and kill him!"

Boots flipped through the pages, shaking his head. "Mark must have gone straight from the cannon to the print shop and worked all night to get this paper out."

Bruno paced the small room like a caged tiger. "He's probably the real Phantom. After we chased him, he got his camera and came back with Fudge and the coach. That's how he can write stuff like this about two guys who are supposed to be his friends!"

"Well, you know Mark and his journalism. He takes the paper really seriously."

Bruno laid both hands flat on the windowsill and gazed at the students hurrying in and out of the Faculty Building. "Even if it isn't Mark," he said angrily, "somebody out there is the real Phantom. And he's letting us hang!"

There was a knock at the door. Boots admitted Larry Wilson.

The office messenger looked worried. "Guys, the heat's on. Everybody says they knew it was you all along. They're taking bets in the cafeteria that you'll be expelled."

All the colour drained from Boots's face. "Expelled?"

"Don't you get it?" cried Larry. "This is no leaf-raking, dishwashing rap! This is the big one!"

"What about the Fish?" asked Bruno. "How's he leaning?"

"It's hard to tell with him," said Larry. "He seems pretty grim, but that might be because he's so sick."

"But do you think he believes us?" asked Boots anxiously.

"It doesn't look good," Larry admitted. "I overheard him putting in a call for Mr. Snow, from the Board of Directors."

"They have to notify the Board if they're expelling any-body!" exclaimed Boots in agony. "My folks are going to kill me!"

"Mine too!" gulped Bruno. "This is a nightmare! This can't happen to people who are innocent!"

"How would we know?" Boots snapped bitterly. "We've never been innocent before!"

Larry opened the door. "I'd better go. The Fish doesn't want anybody to even talk to you. As far as this school is concerned, you guys just died!"

Bruno made a face. "We couldn't get that lucky."

* * *

Mrs. Sturgeon had real tears in her eyes. "I refuse to believe a word of it!"

"They were caught outright, Mildred," her husband explained reasonably, sawing at his steak. "Walton even had the feather in his hand. It's the proverbial 'smoking gun.'"

"Fiddlesticks!" snapped his wife, the fork in her hand shaking. "If Bruno and Melvin say they're innocent, then they are!"

"What those boys say is obviously not worth the air it takes to blow it out their lungs," the Headmaster stated flatly. "Alex Flynn caught them with that mannequin inserted in our cannon." He frowned. "And on top of it all, that dummy was wearing my new hat!"

"Well, that's the proof right there!" Mrs. Sturgeon cried triumphantly. "There's no way for them to get your hat, so they *must* be innocent."

"I'm afraid you're a poor attorney," he replied with a sad smile. "I might have left it at the office; their friend Wilson might have filched it for them. There are dozens of explanations." He looked at his wife earnestly. "I know you mean well, Mildred, and I always value your comments. But this is one instance when I must ask you not to interfere. Expulsion is a very serious internal school matter."

His wife turned pale. "You're going to *expel* them? For a dummy in the cannon?"

Mr. Sturgeon pushed his plate away, virtually untouched. "For a pattern of misbehaviour that flies in the face of everything Macdonald Hall stands for. I gave Walton and O'Neal several chances to confess their identity as our 'phantom.' Each and every time, they chose to lie. I would be grossly remiss in my duties as Headmaster to let that go unpunished."

Mrs. Sturgeon jumped to her feet. "You're just irritable because that confounded toe keeps getting worse! This is Bruno and Melvin you're talking about. Those boys have gone to bat for this school a dozen times! If it weren't for their loyalty, this campus would be covered with condominiums! And don't you try to deny it!"

The Headmaster looked unhappy. "If you think I'm enjoying this, you are sadly mistaken. As unpleasant as this is going to be, it is my job."

Chapter 14

dear nasty uncooperative old goat

Electronics experts from SectorWatch Inc. swarmed over Miss Scrimmage's school like worker ants. They were everywhere — at the doors and windows, on the roof, in the basement and even at the fence and surrounding property. Hammering was heard, and drilling. Wires stretched everywhere like spaghetti. Walls were opened and plastered shut again. Panic buttons and control panels appeared out of nowhere. Huge alarm bullhorns were installed every 15 metres in the hallways. A fifty-thousand-watt floodlight was mounted on the roof of the building.

"I've got to hand it to you, lady," the crew chief was telling Miss Scrimmage. "Of all the security systems on the market, you picked the Rolls Royce. The Fortress

Ultra-Deluxe with Banshee II alarm siren. A *grasshopper* couldn't get into your school undetected."

Miss Scrimmage beamed. In her mind, she was composing a letter to Mr. Sturgeon:

Dear Nasty Uncooperative Old Goat,

This is to advise you and your students to stay
away from my school once and for all . . .

Of course, it would be unladylike to *send* such a letter, but it was pleasant to think about it.

The crew chief looked at his watch. "We should be out of your hair pretty soon. The guys are double-checking the wiring on the doors and windows. Then we can test the system. Not the alarm, of course!" he added hastily.

"But if you don't test the alarm, how do you know it's working?" asked Miss Scrimmage.

"Oh, we have gauges that tell us everything," the man replied airily. "Believe me, you don't want to hear the alarm unless it's absolutely necessary."

A SectorWatch technician approached, dragging Rex by the collar. "This fellow will have to be tied up at night, ma'am."

"Oh, dear," said Miss Scrimmage. "The girls won't like that. He's become a great favourite of theirs."

"Sorry," the man said seriously. "He could trip the motion sensors."

"Oh, well," sighed the Headmistress. "If Rex had been a better watchdog, none of this would have been necessary." She regarded the animal's rotund body critically. "He does seem to have put on a some weight recently."

The crew chief laughed. "That's what happens when you turn a watchdog into a lapdog. He gets fat."

Diane Grant stood at the window of her room, staring at the system of wires that had just been installed there.

Cathy breezed in, waving a thick, red pamphlet. "Well, I managed to get my hands on the operating manual," she said glumly. "Read it and weep."

"I don't have to read it," replied Diane. "I just had one of the workmen explain to me how we're not allowed to open our window ever again."

"Oh, there's a way," said Cathy, leafing through the booklet. "But first I think we have to get Miss Scrimmage to phone up the SectorWatch main monitoring centre in Oshkosh, Wisconsin, and get them to take our room out of the loop."

Diane groaned. "The scariest part is that all the technicians are telling you how it works and how safe you are. But when you ask about the alarm, they get real nervous and change the subject."

Cathy shrugged. "I suppose it's loud. Big deal. Our problem is once that system goes active, we're trapped like dogs here! We can't open the doors or the windows, we can't get to the basement or the roof. And according to this book, the whole property is criss-crossed with little laser beams. If a moving figure breaks the beams, it sets off the alarm. Our whole lifestyle is in danger! We'll be like prisoners in the Black Hole of Calcutta!"

"Well, it's all your fault, Cathy Burton," Diane retorted hotly. "It was your stupid booby traps that convinced Miss Scrimmage to turn this place into Alcatraz!"

There was a tap at the door, and the SectorWatch field manager stuck his head inside. "Hi, girls. I'm just checking to see that your window's been connected. Are you ready for the big test?"

Cathy brightened. "Oh, neat. We're finally going to hear the famous alarm."

The man blanched. "Oh, no. We never set off the alarm on purpose. Not when there are people around."

Diane looked blank. "What's the point of having an alarm if there's no one to hear it?"

"Oh, you'll hear it," the field manager promised grimly. "No doubt about that."

"Well, have *you* ever heard it?" Diane persisted.

"Oh, lots of times!" the man blustered.

"Really?" Cathy probed.

"Well — once. And I was a couple of klicks away. And it was only a Banshee I, whereas you have the new, improved Banshee II — "

"And was it loud?" asked Diane.

"I – I gotta go." And he slipped out of the room. They could hear his footsteps hurrying down the hall.

"In other words," sighed Cathy, "we've got no hope that Miss Scrimmage might just sleep through the alarm."

Diane looked scared. "Cathy, I don't think the *dead* could sleep through the alarm!"

* * *

The cool fall weather continued sunny, but a black cloud hung over room 306 in Dormitory 3. For the next two days, Bruno and Boots lived in limbo. They attended no classes and ate their meals in the kitchen, away from the other students, who were not permitted to associate with them. Making the situation all the more uncomfortable was the knowledge that even this was only temporary.

Their true fate was being decided in the office, or maybe even in the Directors' boardroom in Toronto.

"I envy you," sighed Elmer Drimsdale, who had snuck into their room for a visit.

"*Envy* us?" Boots cried in dismay. "Are you crazy? We're probably going to get expelled!"

"Yes, but you lived on the edge!" declared Elmer. "You challenged the world, neck or nothing! You grabbed the gusto — "

"But we're innocent!" protested Bruno. "We got framed!"

"Guilt or innocence doesn't matter when you live on the edge," Elmer enthused. "I used to do the safe thing and follow every rule."

"Well, you're here to see us," Bruno pointed out. "That's against the rules."

"Because now I'm living on the edge too!" Elmer crowed, eyes blazing. "I'm *glad* Marylou Beakman rejected me! It was my wake-up call! And exactly what I needed to win her back!" He began to pace the room, waxing philosophical. "I used to think the two of you were crazy, the way you snuck out at night, and had fun, and followed your own code. I was so terrified the times you made me go along with you — you must have thought I was an idiot then."

"No," sighed Boots. "We think you're an idiot now! You're risking a lot of trouble for no good reason."

"Like you did!" shrieked Elmer, throwing his arms wide. "Even though you're about to be expelled, I salute you!" He drew himself up to attention, snapped a rigid military salute and held it.

"Aw, come on, Elm," begged Bruno. "Cut it out. This is embarrassing."

But Elmer would have none of it. He stood there, frozen in time, waiting to be saluted back.

Feeling ridiculous, Bruno and Boots got to their feet, faced their visitor and saluted in return.

Elmer dropped his hand. "May we meet again under more pleasant circumstances," he said emotionally. Then he turned on his heel and was gone.

Bruno watched him disappear amidst the crowd of students who were coming out of their rooms carrying armloads of books.

Mr. Fudge's stern voice reached him. "Shut that door, Walton. You're not supposed to be out here."

Bruno obeyed, once again closing room 306 away from the daily life of Macdonald Hall. "I never thought I'd miss classes," he murmured glumly. "I even miss the Fish."

"Well, I don't," said Boots feelingly. "He's probably signing our death warrants right now."

Bruno cocked his head. "Maybe not. The Fish is a pretty fair guy. If anyone's going to believe us, it'll be him."

"Get real, Bruno. He's already put in a call to the Board of Directors."

"Well, maybe that was just a social call," Bruno suggested hopefully, "to — you know — shoot the breeze."

"You're a dreamer," said Boots mournfully.

They were interrupted by a tapping sound at the window. There, crouched in the bushes, was Edward O'Neal.

"Just when I thought things couldn't get worse," groaned Bruno.

"He enjoyed it so much when we were on kitchen duty," said Boots bitterly. "This will flip his cookies." He glared at his brother in the window. "Go away!"

120

But Edward had already raised the sash and had one leg inside.

"You're not supposed to be here, Edward!" Boots hissed, hauling his brother the rest of the way into the room. "How are Mom and Dad going to feel when we *both* show up on the doorstep, bounced out of school?"

"I figured you could use some moral support," said Edward.

"Who from?" asked Boots cynically.

"If Mom and Dad have to come and get you," said Edward, "I'll go with you to meet them. I'll make sure they know all sides of the story."

"What's the catch?" called Bruno. "Blood? Money? A kidney?"

Edward ignored him and regarded his brother intently. "No matter what happens, you can count on me." His smile was open and sincere. "I really hope you don't get expelled. I've been thinking about it a lot. It's nice to have someone around to come and count my shirts."

Boots flushed, recalling how he and Bruno had bullied Edward while searching for a jersey with the mysterious crest on it. "I guess that was pretty mean," he mumbled.

"I'd better go," said Edward, glancing at the clock on Bruno's night table. "I'm late for history. Let me know as soon as you hear anything from the Fish." He exited via the window, and ran off toward the Faculty Building.

"Well, what do you know?" breathed Boots. "My brother's not such a bad guy after all."

"Oh, sure," said Bruno. "Just remember that this sweet supportive little brother of yours could be the real Phantom."

"I forgot." Boots sat down at his desk. "But he seemed so sincere — "

"Maybe that's his guilty conscience. The Phantom is waltzing away, scot-free, leaving you and me hanging on a meat hook!"

Chapter 15

shot at dawn

Larry got the word first: Bruno and Boots were to present themselves at the Headmaster's office at eight the next morning.

"Great," said Bruno, who shunned early hours whenever he could. "We're being shot at dawn."

"I don't even care anymore," said Boots in a small voice. "At this point, it's the waiting that's killing me."

A small group had gathered in room 306 after lights-out. Larry, Wilbur, Sidney and Pete sat in the dark with Bruno and Boots. A flashlight illuminated a printed piece of paper. It was the latest betting line from the dining hall:

Suspended: 5 to 1
Expelled: Even Money
Let off the Hook: 46 to 1

"Forty-six to one!" mourned Bruno. "Doesn't *anybody* think we have a chance?"

"I do," piped up Pete.

"Really?" asked Boots.

Pete hung his head. "Well — no, not really. I just wanted to make you guys feel better."

"The thing that kills me," said Boots, "is that we don't even know who to be mad at. Is my brother being nice, or is he covering up the fact that he's the *real* Phantom? Is Mark guilty, or is he just playing super journalist? And surely Cathy and Diane wouldn't let us take the fall if *they're* the Phantom." He threw up his arms in despair. "But they have no way of knowing what's happening to us!"

"Then there's Marylou Beakman's boyfriend," Larry took up the list. "And whoever was wearing the shirt with the crest on it."

Sidney set his jaw. "One thing we *can* do for you guys is continue the investigation. And when I get my hands on the real Phantom — "

"What are you going to do?" challenged Wilbur. "Bleed on him?"

Nobody laughed.

"*I'm* going to get this guy," said Bruno determinedly, "if it takes me the rest of my life!"

Larry folded his arms in front of him. "I don't care how sick the Fish is. I'm really mad at him for this. He didn't have to *expel* you."

The word hung in the air in front of them.

Pete broke the silence, his voice a whisper. "It's going to be pretty lousy at Macdonald Hall without you guys around."

Larry nodded sadly. "Without Bruno and Boots, Macdonald Hall is just another third-rate school."

"No way!" cried Bruno emotionally, leaping to his feet. "The Hall is *still* the best school in the country! I don't care what happens! Nobody's going to get away with putting down *my* school!"

"It's not going to be your school anymore, Bruno," Boots reminded him gently.

Bruno sat down gloomily on the edge of his bed, propping his chin up with his palms. "It'll always be *sort* of my school," he said, his voice hoarse.

* * *

In the last two days there had been a lot of talk about expulsion — about how it goes on a permanent record, about how it makes finding a new school difficult, about whose parents were going to kill whom. Stuck alone in their room, Bruno and Boots had discussed all the angles of getting expelled — except one. It was the worst thing by far about leaving Macdonald Hall, but the subject was buried like a terrible family secret.

Both of them thought of it. Each could almost sense it in the back of the other's mind. But nothing was said until the two boys stood on the steps of the Faculty Building, bleary-eyed and petrified, steeling themselves for the meeting with Mr. Sturgeon that could be their last.

"You know, Bruno," Boots began bravely. "If we get — you know — sent home, well, you'll be in your town, I'll be in mine. I mean, we probably won't ever see each other again."

"What are you talking about?" blustered Bruno. "Haven't you ever heard of visiting?"

"Think," Boots persisted. "This isn't summer vacation. We're getting expelled. Our folks are probably going to think we're a bad influence on each other. I doubt they're going to be moving heaven and earth to get us together again."

Bruno had no answer. "Maybe it won't be that way." He looked at his watch. "Seven fifty-eight. A hundred and twenty seconds to zero hour."

Boots pushed open the heavy door. "Let's get it over with."

The outer office was deserted. For a moment, Boots toyed with the idea that Mr. Sturgeon had forgotten the meeting. Then he spotted the cane hanging over the half-open wooden door marked HEADMASTER.

"Good morning, boys," came a grim voice from inside.

Boots had been expecting the Headmaster's famous steely grey stare, but what he saw caught him off guard. Seated behind his imposing desk, Mr. Sturgeon looked not furious but sad and tired.

This time Bruno and Boots didn't take their usual place on the bench. They stood before their Headmaster like marines, hands behind their backs.

Mr. Sturgeon regarded them for what seemed like an eternity. "I want you boys to know that what is about to happen to you is not about any prank or practical joke. It is about character, honesty and the willingness to face up to what you have done." He sighed. "I am not the dodder-ing old fool you must think I am. I have always been aware of the potential for mischief you boys possess. But because your misadventures came about in the pursuit of school spirit, albeit misguided, I made it a point to look the other way." He grimaced. "This time, however, I placed my trust in you, and you lied to me. That is no youthful antic. That speaks to character."

Bruno spoke up. "Sir, I know it looks bad, but we *really* didn't do it. We're not the Phantom — "

"I cannot tell you how disappointed I am that you try to deceive me even now," the Headmaster interrupted. "That is why I must regretfully inform you" — he took a deep breath and mopped his brow with a handkerchief — "that you are expelled forthwith from Macdonald Hall."

Both boys flinched as though from a sudden blast of gale-force wind. Here it was, the final judgment. Their deepest fears had come true. They were being thrown out.

Boots looked over at Bruno, waiting for his roommate to protest. *Come on, Bruno!* Boots tried to will his friend to say something, *anything!* After all their adventures at Macdonald Hall, they were going down without a fight, slack-jawed and silent in the Fish's office!

His agonized thoughts were interrupted by a commotion in the outer office. Excited shouts were followed by running footsteps and an enormous crash. The heavy oak door flew open, and in exploded Larry Wilson. His hair was flying, his eyes were wild and he was panting from an all-out sprint through the Faculty Building.

"Mr. Sturgeon! Mr. Sturgeon!"

The Headmaster turned cold, fishy eyes on his office messenger. "When I am in a meeting, I am *not* to be interrupted. You know that, Wilson."

Larry was jumping up and down, babbling. "But — but — somebody just set off firecrackers in the waffle mix at breakfast!"

"This can wait — " said Mr. Sturgeon in annoyance.

"But it was *right now!* Just a minute ago — "

Mr. Sturgeon stood up. "Wilson, that will do — "

"*This* was in the mix, too!" Larry blurted. He stuck out his fist. Clutched in it, dripping batter, was a brown feather.

"The Phantom!" gasped Bruno.

Boots found his voice at last. "It couldn't have been us, sir! We were here, sir! Here with you!" He added, "Right, sir?"

The Headmaster gazed long and hard at the dripping feather. "It would seem that you boys have an airtight alibi."

"We weren't lying, sir," Boots said sincerely. "I know we get in trouble a lot, but we wouldn't do *that.*"

The Headmaster leaned back and steepled his fingers. "You two must have had a very trying few days," he commented quietly. "I do apologize for that."

"Well, I guess we kind of brought it on ourselves, sir," Bruno admitted. "We looked pretty guilty. I'm not sure I would have believed us."

"Even so," said the Headmaster humbly, "I feel terrible about what almost happened. You have the right to know it."

Boots looked up, his face full of hope. "We're not expelled, then?"

"You are not," confirmed Mr. Sturgeon. He nodded toward Larry, who was shuffling in the doorway. "You are dismissed, Wilson. You may go and fulfil your role as town crier. I'm sure the other boys are awaiting word."

Larry raced off to spread the good news.

The Headmaster turned back to Bruno and Boots. "Now that I have apologized, there is something more you have to hear. Boys, things are going to change. You are both familiar with the rule book, and you know its pages are not filled with advertising. Three days ago, you were caught on the front lawn, under suspicious circumstances, in the middle of the night. I do not intend to punish you, since I feel you've been punished enough. But for your own sake, for my sake, for the sake of Macdonald Hall — observe the curfew!" He glared at them. "You may go."

The Headmaster of Macdonald Hall maintained his stern expression as Bruno and Boots left the office. It wasn't until the heavy oak door clicked shut that the grin split his face.

"Yes!" He danced a happy jig, with high kicks. The celebration came to an abrupt end when his sore toe slammed into the desk.

"Yee-owww!!"

Chapter 16

one lousy little broken wire

"Hey, Mr. Wong! How's it going? You're looking sharp! It sure is great to be back in geography class! I hope we didn't miss too much! Need us to do any extra homework to get caught up? Are you sure — hey, Boots, cut it out! Let go! Hey — "

"Bruno," Boots whispered as he hauled his roommate bodily to their seats. "Everybody's staring at us. They're looking at you like you've gone nuts."

"I don't care," Bruno grinned stubbornly. "I'm just too happy about not being expelled to shut up about it." He leaped to his feet. "Guys, I have an announcement to make. Boots and I aren't expelled. So we'll be here from now on."

There was a burst of applause, and Bruno and Boots accepted backslaps and handshakes.

"I hope no one minds if we do a little geography," put in Mr. Wong, handing out a stack of printed pamphlets. He paused in front of Bruno and Boots. "It's good to have you back, Walton — O'Neal."

"Thank you, sir," said Bruno appreciatively. He pulled the top two pamphlets from the pile for himself and Boots.

Boots turned his attention to the booklet on his desk. It was entitled "Mineral Deposits Throughout the World." He stared at the design on the cover, which featured a globe, flattened into an oval. Arranged around it were pictures of molecules. At the very top was an ornate crown. Boots frowned. Mr. Wong had never used these pamphlets before. Why did that picture seem so familiar?

It hit him like a bolt out of the blue — *this was the mysterious crest from the shirt on the videotape!* The flattened globe had appeared to be an egg in the dim light! The molecules provided the circles and the crown they had recognized right from the start!

"Bruno!" he hissed. "Take a look at this!"

"Yeah? So?" Bruno regarded his pamphlet.

"Don't you see it?" Boots persisted. "It's the crest from the video!" Breathlessly, he pointed out the egg, the circles and the crown, tracing the shapes with his pencil.

Bruno's hand shot up. "Mr. Wong! *Mr. Wong!*"

The teacher rolled his eyes. "What is it now, Walton?"

Bruno shook his head. "Sir, I just wanted to know — what's this crest on the cover of the booklet."

"Oh, that's the insignia of the Royal Geophysical Society."

"Thanks." Bruno sat back in confusion. "That doesn't make any sense. What kind of a creep would wear a T-shirt from a Geophysical Society."

The answer came to both of them at the same time. Bruno and Boots snapped to attention, looked at each other and chorused, *"Elmer Drimsdale!"*

* * *

"Elmer is the Phantom?" exclaimed Pete Anderson in disbelief.

"Shhh!" cautioned Bruno, looking around the dining hall to make sure the school genius wasn't within earshot. "I know it sounds crazy, but who else would have a T-shirt from the Royal Geophysical Society?"

"And think how weird he's been acting lately," added Boots. "All this 'living on the edge' stuff."

"Yeah, but the Phantom started out long before Elmer went off his nut," Larry pointed out.

"Maybe not," said Bruno. "Don't forget, Elmer first saw Marylou What's-her-face at the Summer Science Fair. He was sending her those stupid presents three days into school! What if Elmer cooked up this whole Phantom thing because he thought it would make him seem more glamorous to Marylou?"

Wilbur peered over a towering stack of chili nachos. "So why did he lend us the telescope and videocam if he was the Phantom all along?"

"Because he knew we were watching Scrimmage's, and not him." Boots replied readily.

"Here's the crusher," said Bruno. "The Phantom's calling card is a feather, right? Who's got access to a pile of feathers at Macdonald Hall?" He surveyed their faces around the table. "The same guy who got his hands on bird droppings."

"Then he made up a fake boyfriend," said Boots, "so we could suspect *him* instead of Elmer."

"I know it's hard to believe," added Bruno. "But you can't argue with the evidence."

"All that stuff is just coincidence," frowned Larry. "I think we were right the first time. The Phantom is your brother Edward. He's got the ability — I mean, he's rotten enough. He's got the motive — he wants to show us 'old men' who's in charge. And we know he constantly sneaks out at night. What more proof do we need?"

"You guys are nuts," grumbled Wilbur, rearranging the jalapeños on a loaded chip. "This Phantom stuff is coming straight from Scrimmage's. Anybody crazy enough to booby-trap an apple orchard could be the Phantom in her spare time. It's Cathy and Diane."

Sidney shook his head. "It's Mark all the way. You should see him, guys! He's hardly even a friend anymore. He spends all his time at the newspaper, writing articles about the Phantom. Plus he was right there on the scene when Bruno and Boots got caught at the cannon. Trust me. It's Mark."

Pete spoke up. "I think it's George Wexford-Smyth III."

Boots rolled his eyes. "He *graduated* last year."

"Oh," said Pete. "Well then, I guess it has to be one of those other guys."

"We'll know soon enough," said Bruno.

"Wait a minute," said Wilbur, his voice wary. "'Knowing soon enough' almost got you guys expelled."

Bruno smiled brilliantly. "Don't worry about a thing. I have a plan."

There were groans all around.

"We can't find the Phantom," Bruno explained, "but we can make the Phantom find us."

"Quit talking in riddles," growled Wilbur. "Spit it out."

"We'll set a trap," supplied Boots.

Larry was unconvinced. "Using what for bait?"

"What else?" grinned Bruno. "A practical joke — a joke so perfect, *no one* could resist!"

* * *

Mr. Sturgeon was adjusting the ice pack on his sore toe when his wife raced in.

"William, I told you so!" she cried triumphantly.

The Headmaster stared straight ahead. "I have absolutely no idea what you mean," he said stubbornly.

"Bruno and Melvin," she insisted. "I *told* you they were innocent! I *told* you they wouldn't lie!"

Mr. Sturgeon's features softened. "You cannot imagine how relieved I am," he admitted. "I was *this* close to sending for their parents."

"Macdonald Hall has put those poor boys through torture this week," Mrs. Sturgeon scolded. "Confined to their room, not knowing whether or not they were going to be expelled — I hope you made them a proper apology!"

The Headmaster nodded. "I tried. But bear in mind, Mildred, that *not* being the Phantom doesn't excuse them for their rampage of rule-breaking. As remorseful as I was feeling, I could not exactly bring myself to give them a medal."

"Well, thank heaven nothing terrible happened." She moved behind his chair and placed her hands on his shoulders. "I'm sorry, William. I've been so concerned about those poor boys that I never considered how hard this must have been on you."

"It's all in a day's work, Mildred," her husband sighed. "I enjoy the celebrations but I carry the burdens as well."

Mrs. Sturgeon patted him comfortingly. "Well, it won't be for much longer," she reassured him.

He turned to look at her. "Whatever do you mean?"

"Why, William — you're retiring at the end of this year."

The Headmaster straightened up in his chair. "I most certainly am not!"

She looked bewildered. "But you said — "

"This institution needs me more now that it ever did," Mr. Sturgeon declared stoutly. "A crazed practical joker wreaks havoc on my campus! That deranged woman across the street is installing a security system with everything but antiaircraft guns — no doubt our students will soon be caught up in it! Two innocent boys came perilously close to being expelled! Can't you see it, Mildred? I am the only anchor of sanity in the rough seas of chaos!" He glanced at his watch. "Even as we speak, I'm late for a staff meeting!" He hobbled toward the door, hopping into his sock and muttering under his breath, "Retirement! That'll be the day!"

If he had bothered to turn around, he would have seen that his wife was smiling.

* * *

Diane flipped helplessly through the SectorWatch Fortress Ultra-Deluxe technical manual. "Cathy, I really don't see what you expect me to do."

Cathy paced the room, snapping a pencil into halves and quarters. "Do *something!* Anything! The security system goes on in two minutes and we'll be trapped like rats in here! We can't get out — the guys can't get in — we'll have to follow the *rules!*"

"I wonder what that's like," Diane mused.

"Trust me. It stinks!" snapped Cathy. "We can't let SectorWatch turn on the system. We've got to stop it — dismantle it — bust it — kill it!"

"It's impossible," argued Diane. "You have to be an engineer to understand this manual. Hey — where are you going?"

Cathy had heaved the door open and was about to fling herself out into the corridor. "I don't know! To bang my head against the wall! To go berserk in a wider area! To challenge Rex to a growling contest!" She lunged forward.

There was a snapping noise and all at once she was tripping, tumbling, rolling down the hall. Diane raced after her. "Cathy, are you okay?"

"I tripped over something!" Cathy gasped.

Both girls looked back to the doorway. From the small gap where the pink carpet of the room met the sturdy shag of the hall, something was sticking up. The two crawled over to investigate. The frayed, broken ends of two pieces of wire protruded from under the broadloom.

Diane frowned. "I wonder what you ripped."

The answer came over the P.A. system. *"Warning,"* announced a computerized voice. *"There is an interruption in the SectorWatch system. The Fortress Ultra-Deluxe will not arm."*

It dawned on Cathy slowly, and her expression turned from surprise to delight to pure joy.

"Amazing," she breathed. "All this space-age technology

and one lousy little broken wire shuts the whole thing down!"

"Shouldn't we tell somebody?" asked Diane nervously.

"I'll tell you and you'll tell me and we'll both know," Cathy replied, stuffing the two broken wires under the rug. "Get the Elmer's glue. If we get the carpet back in place, with luck, no one will ever find this!"

* * *

Bruno and Boots knocked on the door of room 342, down the hall from their own room.

Tall, blond Chris Talbot appeared. "Hey, guys," he greeted. "Congratulations on not getting expelled."

He ushered them inside the room, which was one of the most impressive at Macdonald Hall. Chris's paintings and sketches covered the walls; sculptures of all sizes stood on pedestals, shelves and furniture, along with the many trophies, ribbons and prizes on display. Chris was Macdonald Hall's most promising young art student.

Bruno got right down to business. "We need a favour."

Chris laughed. "I didn't think you were here to clean my bathroom. What's up?"

"We want to set a trap for the Phantom," Boots explained.

Chris's eyebrows rose. "How can you do that? You can never predict where he's going to strike next."

Bruno sat down on the edge of Chris's desk. "You know how when you see wet cement, you just can't resist putting your initials in it? That's the kind of guy the Phantom is. He sees a cannon and he wants to stuff something in it. He sees a statue and he wants to dress it up. We need a poster to tempt him like that — a picture so irresistible, so perfect, that the Phantom won't be able to stand it if he doesn't sneak over and draw something on it."

"Well," Chris said thoughtfully, "I told Coach Flynn I'd do the poster for the big indoor track meet down in Toronto. I'll show you my preliminary sketches."

He spread the drawings out on the bed. "What do you think?"

Bruno's eyes widened in delight. "Perfect!" he crowed. "The first thing we need is a big piece of paper — and I mean big!"

Chapter 17

the discus thrower

SectorWatch Inc. sent a team of troubleshooters to locate the glitch in Miss Scrimmage's security system. Six technicians combed the school, searching for the one trouble spot that was keeping the Fortress Ultra-Deluxe off-line.

They began by checking all the fuse and junction boxes for broken circuits. They found nothing. The next step was a thorough examination of all the door and window connections. Everything was secure.

"Oh, good," said Miss Scrimmage. "So there's nothing wrong."

"Well, not exactly," the crew chief admitted. "We know there's a break in the loop but we don't know where it is."

Miss Scrimmage looked alarmed. "My word, what shall we do?"

He smiled kindly. "Don't worry. We'll find it. But first we have to shut down everything."

"Gracious! Why?"

The chief's eyes widened. "Why? That kind of tinkering could set off the *alarm!*"

"Well," chided Miss Scrimmage, "that's not the end of the world."

"No," said the man through clenched teeth. "It just sounds like it."

Miss Scrimmage tittered. "Oh, you fellows are so full of fun."

Cathy and Diane also watched the progress of the work crew, Cathy in amusement, and her roommate in growing panic.

"Cathy, this is *horrible,*" she quavered. "Those poor workmen have been tearing the whole school apart for hours, and we could show them the problem in three seconds!"

Cathy shrugged. "They get paid."

"That's not the point," Diane insisted. "This is *wrong!*"

Cathy smiled serenely. "What's *wrong* is keeping three hundred tender young ladies in a prison camp. So if they *never* find that broken wire, it'll be too soon for me."

She watched benignly as a technician crawled down the hall, training a flashlight along the baseboard, following the wire that was stapled there.

"Hi, ma'am," Cathy greeted the young woman warmly. "I just got a package from home. Want a cookie?"

The technician looked up and smiled. "Yeah, thanks."

She savoured the chocolate chip cookie and accepted another. "These are delicious. Your mom's a great cook."

"I'll tell her," said Cathy. Actually, this stash had been baked in Miss Scrimmage's kitchen and was destined for Rex. "'Bye."

When the technician resumed her painstaking check of the loop, she began on the other side of their door — past the break in the wire that the girls had concealed under the carpet.

* * *

In the main foyer of the Faculty Building, Wilbur and Boots held the top of the giant art board and Chris Talbot unrolled his poster.

Bruno gawked. "It's beautiful! It's *perfect!*"

TORONTO INDOOR TRACK & FIELD MEET
SKYDOME DECEMBER 4 & 5

. . . blazoned the heading in big, red letters.

Below this was a painting of the famous Greek statue of the Discus Thrower. The nude marble figure was viewed from behind and it was definitely not Chris's best work. This was as per Bruno's instructions. The artist had deliberately drawn the hips more than twice the normal size. The result was that the Discus Thrower was positively pear-shaped, with a gigantic hind end that seemed to stare back at the viewer.

Wilbur emitted a low whistle. "Man, check out the size of that butt! It looks like the back end of an aircraft carrier!"

"It's colossal!" agreed Boots with reverence.

Wilbur regarded Chris questioningly. "I thought the Discus Thrower was supposed to be an athlete. He looks like he trains on cheesecake! You could rent out advertising space on that derrière!"

Chris laughed and pointed at Bruno. "Ask the boss."

Bruno's eyes gleamed. "If the Phantom is *half* the joker he thinks he is, there's no way he'll be able to resist drawing something on this!" He turned to gaze at the Discus Thrower. "I can hardly resist it myself!"

"Down, boy," said Boots as though he were training a dog. "This is our trap for the Phantom, remember?"

"Awww!" moaned Bruno. "Couldn't I just put *Eat at Joe's* and then erase it?"

"Or how about a big smiling face?" suggested Wilbur. "With *Have a Nice Day* written underneath."

"Come on," cautioned Chris. "I'm going to catch a lot of flak from Coach Flynn over this. The least you can do is keep your mitts off it and let the Phantom get there first."

Boots frowned worriedly. "I hope the Phantom gets his chance at it. The minute we put this up, every guy in school is going to want to scribble his initials on it."

"They'd fit," confirmed Wilbur.

"Look who's talking," Chris told him.

The office door opened and Mr. Sturgeon hobbled out, assisted by his wife. He stared at the poster, his eyes becoming wide behind his steel-rimmed glasses. "Goodness," he said in a faint voice. "What a healthy specimen!"

Mrs. Sturgeon smiled brilliantly. "It's wonderfully impressive, like all your work, Christopher. Congratulations."

His face red, Chris tried to mumble his thanks.

"Sir, are you okay?" asked Bruno seriously. "I think your limp is getting worse."

"Not at all, Walton," Mr. Sturgeon grimaced in pain. "I am fit as — ah, Mr. Flynn!" he exclaimed, grateful to change the subject.

Coach Flynn jogged into the building. "Good morning, everybody. I can't wait to see Talbot's new poster for the — whoa!" He caught sight of the Discus Thrower and stopped dead in his tracks.

"Great, isn't it?" Bruno enthused.

"What? Oh, yeah — great," the coach managed in a strangled voice. "Only, why is it so — you know — like that?"

The question hung in the air.

Chris was the first to break the silence. "You're disappointed?" he asked in hurt tones.

"No!" the coach said quickly. "I love it! It's — larger than life!"

The Macdonald Hall students thought so, too. All through the school day, the poster was surrounded by an appreciative audience of pointers and laughers. "Get a load of the caboose on that guy!"

"The Hindenberg!"

"I'm quitting track and field! I don't want to end up looking like that!"

Elmer Drimsdale provided the scientific opinion. "This is anatomically impossible."

Edward O'Neal seemed unimpressed, as usual. "Big deal," he yawned. "A discus."

"This is unbearable," grimaced poor Chris. "I didn't know

there were this many wisecracks in the language!"

"It's perfect!" crowed Bruno. "Every guy in the school is going to hear about that poster — *including* the Phantom. He's as good as caught!"

* * *

Just after lights-out that night, the window of room 306 opened and two shadowy figures dropped to the shrubbery below.

Keeping low, Bruno and Boots dashed across the campus to the deserted Faculty Building.

"So much for the Fish's big curfew speech," whispered Boots. "After all this, I sure hope the Phantom hasn't been here already and we've missed him."

They slipped inside. A single light at the back of the hallway illuminated the poster. It was untouched. The broad backside of the Discus Thrower gleamed out at them.

"It looks even bigger in the dark," Bruno admired.

"Where are we going to hide?" asked Boots nervously.

Bruno's eyes lit on the big lost and found chest that sat near the entrance to the office area. He lifted the hinged lid. "After you, Melvin."

The two settled themselves amidst the scarves, gloves, books and shoes. Bruno lowered the lid, propping it open in the corner with a tennis shoe. That left a four-centimetre gap, through which the boys peered. There was a clear view of the poster.

"What now?" asked Boots.

"We wait," said Bruno. "Just don't fall asleep. I can really picture us trying to explain this to the Fish when he finds us tomorrow morning."

In the gloom of room 201, a match flared. A trembling hand touched the flame to a candlewick and the light swelled, bringing the walls to life in the dim glow. A drip of wax splashed onto the pile of books strewn every which way on the desk — *Introduction to Skydiving, Climb Mount Everest, The Encyclopedia of Daredevils* and the latest issue of *Soldier of Fortune* magazine. An instructional video, *Wing-Walking for Beginners,* lay on a stack of order forms from the Music-by-Mail Record Club.

Elmer Drimsdale, dressed in jeans and a black turtle-neck, pulled a dark stocking cap down over his fair crew cut.

He paused for a moment and took several deep breaths. What he was about to do terrified him, but that was part of living on the edge. "One cannot stay in one's room and play it safe all the time," he mumbled to himself. He was going for the gusto!

With a flourish of his pen, he chose two more albums on the order form, snuffed the candle and eased himself out the small window into the bushes. The cool night air set his heart pounding. He felt scared but alive. This was it! Tonight he would do it!

Chapter 18

the shadow of the phantom

Cathy and Diane shinnied down the drainpipe outside their window and jumped to the ground.

"You see?" Cathy was saying. "If we hadn't busted that little wire, there's no way we could be doing this. Just opening our window would have set off the alarm."

"And we never, *never* set off the alarm on purpose," the two girls chanted and laughed.

"Well, we'd better enjoy our freedom while it lasts," giggled Diane. "Tomorrow that special team of SectorWatch experts arrives from Wisconsin. They're sure to find your little broken wire."

Cathy dismissed this. "I can't take these guys seriously anymore. What a bunch of big babies, scared to death of a little noise! Maybe I'll just threaten to set off the alarm and they'll all hightail it to the North Pole!"

"Shhh!" Diane grabbed her roommate by the arm and dragged her into the shadows of the apple orchard. "Someone's coming!"

They listened as furtive footsteps crunched in the dry leaves. Then a slim silhouette loomed up out of the darkness.

Cathy's brow knit. "It's not Bruno or Boots — too skinny."

Diane whimpered in fear. "Now look what you've done! You've disabled the SectorWatch and this is a *real intruder!*"

"Hmmm," said Cathy.

"What are we going to *do?*" Diane squeaked.

"Prepare to defend our school," Cathy declared grimly.

As the figure rounded the corner of the building, she launched herself forward like a CFL linebacker. She hit the intruder just below the knees, knocking his legs out from under him. Then, as he collapsed to the ground, Diane struck, jumping on the prostrate victim with windmilling arms.

The struggle continued until the girls heard a familiar voice: "But at least I lived on the edge!"

The girls froze. *"Elmer?"* they chorused.

The Macdonald Hall school genius sat up and adjusted his glasses.

"Oh, hi," said Cathy, as though she were greeting someone at a tea party. "What brings you here?"

"I live on the edge now," Elmer croaked.

"The edge of what?" asked Diane.

A dry rattle came from Elmer. His throat usually closed up in the presence of girls. But he realized he would have to overcome that.

"I've been timid for too long," Elmer replied in a strong voice that surprised even him. "I've come to meet Marylou Beakman face to face."

They looked blank. "Why?"

Elmer turned three shades of red. "That's personal," he said stiffly.

"Ooooooooh!" chorused the girls. It came out as a seven-syllable word.

"You and Marylou Beakman!" Cathy exclaimed. "Cool!"

"You guys would make the perfect couple!" Diane enthused.

"Well, it's somewhat complicated," Elmer admitted. "I'm not yet one hundred percent sure that Marylou likes me. You see, I sent her two very nice gifts and I never heard from her at all."

Instantly, Cathy was alert. "Gifts? What kind of gifts?"

"Very superior specimens," Elmer replied. "A rare rodent skull and the droppings of the Tasmanian Mountain Sparrow."

It hit the girls at the same time. The threatening packages that had so frightened Marylou and Miss Scrimmage! The voodoo curse had been no curse at all — just a love token from Elmer Drimsdale!

It was too much. The girls collapsed into each other's arms and howled with laughter.

Elmer was outraged. "Those gifts came from the heart!"

But Cathy and Diane were out of control. They threw

themselves to the ground and rolled amidst the leaves, hysterical.

"Oh, so you think this is amusing!" Elmer exclaimed in great anger. "Well, it is not! Romance can be a deeply painful matter!"

Cathy struggled to compose herself. "Sorry, Elmer," she managed, still shaking. "We didn't mean any harm."

"You're a great guy," added Diane. "I can't understand why Marylou didn't go gaga over your presents."

Elmer's face radiated deep tragedy. "I'm afraid I can," he said sombrely. "I believe Marylou Beakman already has a boyfriend."

Cathy thought it over. Marylou was one of the quietest, dullest, most ordinary girls at Scrimmage's. The idea of not one, but two boys after her —

"No way," she said flatly. "Not a chance."

"But I've seen him," Elmer protested. "He gains access to her room via the TV antenna mast outside her window."

Cathy grabbed Elmer with one hand and Diane with the other. "Come on," she said. "Let's settle this once and for all."

* * *

In the darkened Dormitory 1, a window silently rose. A backpack was tossed out into the bushes. Then a leg was thrown over the sill.

Edward O'Neal hopped to the ground and retrieved his backpack. He unzipped it and peered inside. Yes, he had everything he needed.

He passed a cursory glance over the campus. He had been very nervous about doing this at first, but the butterflies in his stomach had long since disappeared. Hey, after getting away with it so many times, what was there to be nervous about?

* * *

In the lost and found box in the Faculty Building, Bruno snored, stretched and kicked Boots in the stomach. Boots snapped awake, sitting up suddenly and banging his head on the lid of the wooden chest.

"What . . . ?" The noise brought Bruno to life.

The two looked at each other in horror. "You were asleep!" they chorused accusingly.

In a panic, they threw open the box and stared at the poster. The Discus Thrower's hind end was unmarked.

"Whew," breathed Bruno. "We didn't miss anything."

A faint scraping sound met their ears.

Boots froze. "What was that?"

Quickly, Bruno eased the lid back down over them. "There's someone on the stairs outside!"

They crouched there, frozen, watching the doorknob turn.

"This is it!" whispered Bruno.

And then the door was open, and a long thin shadow was splashed across the foyer — the shadow, they hoped, of the Phantom.

* * *

Cathy tapped lightly on the door of Marylou Beakman's room. "It may take her a while," she whispered. "She's probably asleep."

But the door opened almost immediately, and it was no sleepy pyjama-clad girl who appeared. Marylou was wide awake and fully dressed, her red hair held neatly back by a bright green headband.

150

"Oh," said Cathy, annoyed. "What are you doing up?"

Marylou laughed. "I could ask you the same question." Her eyes moved beyond the girls and fell on Elmer. "Hey, you're the guy who won the Summer Science Fair. How did you get here?"

"I – I – " Elmer just stood there, sweating and staring.

"Elmer goes to Macdonald Hall," Diane supplied.

Cathy put an arm around Elmer's shoulders. "One of the coolest guys there. Best friends with Bruno and Boots. Why don't you invite us in, and we'll hang out for a while?"

"Well, I — uh — "

But Cathy pushed right past her, and propelled herself, Diane and Elmer into the room.

"I'm kind of busy," said Marylou.

"Hey, how's it going?" Cathy greeted Marylou's roommate.

The sleeping girl rolled over, snoring softly. Cathy turned to Marylou. "When did Teresa lapse into a coma?"

Marylou shuffled uncomfortably. "She's kind of a heavy sleeper."

Elmer had been steeling himself to make a comment, and finally it came: "This is a very impressive room, Marylou. Truly magnificent."

Everyone stared at him. The room was a Xerox copy of every other one at Scrimmage's.

"Uh — thanks," said Marylou uncertainly.

A tap at the window made them all jump. Her face bright red with guilt, Marylou opened the window and grabbed a gloved hand.

Elmer was devastated. "It's her boyfriend!" he whispered to Cathy. "I told you!"

A leg was slung over the sill; a body appeared, then a head.

Cathy gaped. *"Edward?"*

Edward O'Neal looked from the crowd to Marylou. "Did I come on the wrong night?"

Marylou helped him the rest of the way into the room.

Diane was still trying to figure things out. "Edward is Marylou's boyfriend?"

"Boyfriend?" repeated Marylou. "What gave you that idea?"

"It's pretty obvious," said Cathy. "What's he doing here?"

"None of your business!" snapped Edward.

"Oh, yeah?" Cathy snatched up his backpack. With a flick of her wrist, she unzipped it and dumped the contents on the floor: a ruler, protractor, compass, reams of scribbled notes and a thick textbook titled *Geometry*.

Diane frowned. "I don't get it. Who brings his girlfriend math homework?"

Edward stuck out his chin. "She's not my girlfriend! If you must know, I ran into Marylou that first night I came over here. We got to talking and she mentioned she was on the math team. I asked her to help me with geometry so I wouldn't flunk — sue me!"

Elmer spoke up. "But why didn't you come to me? I would have helped you."

"Then my brother would have found out," Edward explained. "And he would have told my mother. So please don't spill the beans."

"I promise," said Elmer. He was so grateful to Edward for not being Marylou's boyfriend, he would have promised anything.

Bruno and Boots watched breathlessly as the long shadow advanced across the Faculty Building floor. Their eyes fixed on the door, they waited for whoever was casting that image.

And suddenly, there was the figure, standing just inside the entrance. The Phantom was dressed all in black, with a dark ski mask covering his face.

Boots's heart was pounding in his throat. He could see the Phantom's eyes through the ski mask. They looked so familiar! His mind worked furiously, but he could not connect those eyes with any of the suspects. One thing, though, was clear; those eyes were focused on the Discus Thrower on the wall.

With swift, light steps, the Phantom breezed past the lost-and-found box and crossed the foyer to Chris Talbot's poster. From a pocket, the figure produced two things: a long brown feather and a magic marker. The feather he laid carefully on the floor under the Discus Thrower. Then he pulled the cap from the marker.

The pen moved forward in a steady hand . . .

"Now!" cried Bruno, hurling back the lid of the wooden box.

Bruno and Boots scrambled out of the lost-and-found and hurled themselves at the Phantom. Both boys were expecting a struggle from the master prankster who had eluded capture for so long. But the Phantom merely stood and allowed Boots to pull his arms behind his back.

Eyes blazing, Bruno stepped out in front of the captive. "So this is the great Phantom," he jeered. "The uncatchable joker, the Houdini of Macdonald Hall. Well, buddy-boy, you are *toast!*"

He reached out and yanked off the ski mask, revealing at last the face of the Phantom.

Bruno's jaw dropped.

Boots released his captive and staggered back, wheezing.

The Phantom cast them a dazzling smile. "Bruno — Melvin."

It was Mrs. Sturgeon!!

Chapter 19

watch out for the lasers

Mr. Sturgeon was normally a sound sleeper — even more so now that he was dosed with pain pills. But in the midst of an elaborate dream, his foot suddenly exploded like a hand grenade. He woke up to a searing pain and the realization that he had rolled over and kicked the bedpost with his sore toe.

He stifled a cry to avoid waking his wife. But when he looked over to make sure she was undisturbed, he noticed that she was not even there.

He sat up. "Mildred?"

There was no answer.

"Mildred — " he called, louder.

Still no reply.

He got out of bed and hobbled to the top of the stairs. *"Mildred!"* he bellowed.

Where was his wife?

Somewhat alarmed, the Headmaster threw on his red silk bathrobe, stepped gingerly into his bedroom slippers and limped down the stairs. He looked out on the porch and scanned the deserted campus. All seemed quiet. Where on earth could she be?

Mr. Sturgeon frowned. He had no idea where to look, but he couldn't just sit here in the house and wait for her to come back from wherever she was. What an odd situation!

He limped to the closet and shrugged into his overcoat. A small feathered hat fell from the top shelf and came to rest on his foot.

"Ugh," he said aloud, picking it up. What an ugly hat. Since when did Mildred have such terrible taste? He snapped his fingers. This wasn't his wife's; this monstrosity belonged to Miss Scrimmage. She had left it here after her first snit of the school year. Idly, he wondered why Mildred had never returned it in all this time.

And — wait a minute. Miss Scrimmage's hat had been covered in feathers. Yet now it was almost naked. What had happened to them?

What use could his wife have for ugly feathers? Long brown ones, the same kind the Phantom —

He dropped the hat as though it had burned his fingers. The unthinkable slammed into his mind with the force of a runaway train. Those were Phantom feathers! Could *Mildred* be the Phantom? It made no sense, but who could deny the evidence?

He grabbed his cane from the umbrella stand. More

than ever now, it was urgent that he find his wife. Where could she be?

He paused at the door. Where would the Phantom be? It came to him with remarkable clarity. Tonight there could be only one target for the legendary practical joker of Macdonald Hall.

The Discus Thrower.

* * *

Elmer walked between Cathy and Diane back to their room. His feet hardly touched the floor. Every few steps, he would launch himself straight up, punching at the air and cheering, "Yes! Yes!"

"Cut it out!" hissed Diane. "You'll wake up Miss Scrimmage!"

"I'm sorry," Elmer struggled to contain himself. "I'm just so jubilant that Marylou doesn't have a boyfriend! I am ebullient! Effervescent! Exultant!"

"You're happy," Cathy translated.

"That too," confirmed the genius. "You know, I think Marylou liked me."

"How could she resist?" groaned Cathy. "I'll tell you what. I'll raid the kitchen and we can chow down while Marylou is tutoring Edward. Then we can go back and you two can get acquainted." She ran off, flashing thumbs-up.

Elmer glowed. "You're great friends. Imagine — I used to think you girls were maniacs."

Diane laughed and unlocked her door. "Now, you've got to promise to stop celebrating. It's the middle of the night."

"I'm sorry," Elmer said again. "I just want the whole world to share in the joy I feel. I want to help people, right wrongs, spread sunshine — " As he danced in behind her, his foot caught under the hastily glued carpet. The edge came loose and flipped up, revealing the broken SectorWatch wire. "Here — I can help you with this." He dropped to his knees, picked up the two broken ends and expertly wound them together.

Diane stared in horror. "Elmer — *no!*"

The P.A. system came to life:

Warning, came the computerized voice. *The SectorWatch system is now armed. This is your thirty-second exit delay.*

Slicing salami in the kitchen, Cathy turned to stone.

Halfway through an isosceles triangle, Marylou and Edward froze.

Miss Scrimmage sat bolt upright in bed.

Diane's face was chalk-white. "Elmer, you idiot! You turned on the security system! You've got thirty seconds to get out of here!"

"But what about Marylou?" Elmer protested.

"If you're not gone in thirty seconds, you're trapped!" Diane shrilled, throwing open the window. "Hurry!"

Miserably, Elmer climbed out and began to ease down the drainpipe. The last thing he heard before the window slammed shut was Diane's whisper: *"And watch out for the lasers!"*

Head spinning, Elmer jumped to the ground.

POW! He collided head-on with a running figure. It was Edward O'Neal, sprinting for home. Both boys collapsed to the ground, dazed.

The P.A. system crackled again: *Warning. The exit delay is now complete. The Banshee II alarm is in full readiness.*

"Let's get out of here!" cried Edward, scrambling to his feet.

"No!" Elmer tackled him and brought him down. "I think the security system has lasers out here! If we break one of the beams, it'll set off the alarm!"

Edward scanned the grounds. "I don't see any lasers."

"The beams are invisible!" Elmer hissed.

Edward threw his arms wide. "If we can't see them, how do we avoid them?"

Elmer's mind worked furiously. He knew so much science! But all of that was useless if he couldn't put a little theory into practice.

He got to his feet, bumping his knee painfully on the tap of Miss Scrimmage's lawn sprinkler system.

"Of course!" he said out loud. He twisted the tap handle. Jets of water began to squirt from dozens of outlets across the lawn. And there they were. The fine spray reflected the narrow beams of the SectorWatch lasers. Elmer and Edward looked out over a network of criss-crossing red lasers stretched out over the lawn like a spider's web.

"Wow!" breathed Edward in awe.

"Follow me," whispered Elmer.

The beams were a half metre off the ground. The two boys flattened themselves to the grass and began to snake their way under the laser web.

* * *

Bruno and Boots stared in mute shock at the wife of their Headmaster.

Bruno found his voice first. "Mrs. Sturgeon — " he barely whispered. "*You're* the Phantom? But — but why? But how?"

She smiled sweetly. "I think I've proved that I have as much of a sense of humour as any of you boys."

"Humour?" blurted Boots. "We almost got expelled over this Phantom stuff!"

"I would never have allowed that to happen," she replied stoutly. "Why do you think I waited until you were in the office before I put the firecrackers in the waffle mix? You were with Mr. Sturgeon. That proved you weren't the Phantom."

"You saved our hides!" breathed Boots.

"All those gags were *nothing* compared with the joke of the Phantom's true identity," Bruno said in admiration. "How did you pull it off?"

She shrugged modestly. "No one suspects the Headmaster's wife. Why, half the kitchen staff was there when I slipped those cherry bombs in the waffle mix. But nobody was watching *me*."

"Amazing," marvelled Boots, shaking his head. "You fooled *everybody!*"

"Not everybody," she corrected ruefully. She indicated the Discus Thrower. "This was a trap all along, wasn't it? You knew your Phantom wouldn't be able to resist it."

Bruno nodded. "Sorry, ma'am. In a million years, we never dreamed it was going to be you."

"It was brilliant," she said approvingly. "I'm very proud of you. As soon as I saw the expanse of that magnificent posterior, I knew it was my next job."

"Ma'am?" ventured Boots. "What happens now? Are you still going to be the Phantom?"

"Oh, no. The Phantom is hanging up his feathers as of tonight." She stepped forward, pen at the ready. "This is my last caper."

The boys watched with bated breath as she began to

draw on the poster. Then she stepped away and there it was, written across the broad backside of the Discus Thrower: GOODYEAR.

Bruno clapped his hands like a small child in a toy store. "That's perfect!"

Even Boots had to smile. "Nice one, ma'am."

There was the sound of someone outside on the front steps. The three froze and listened. The pace was uneven, like a limp, and there was the *thump, thump, thump* that could only be a cane.

All the colour drained out of Boots's face. "It's the Fish!" He stared in horror at Mrs. Sturgeon. "I mean — uh — your husband! Bruno . . . " How could they turn Mrs. Sturgeon in? She had always stuck up for them, been their friend in the worst of times. What if Mr. Sturgeon never forgave her? A forty-year marriage could go down the drain!

Bruno read his thoughts. "You're right."

With one mind, the two boys hustled Mrs. Sturgeon over to the lost-and-found box and stuffed her inside amidst the coats and scarves. They slammed down the lid a split second before the Headmaster limped onto the scene, grim-faced.

"Walton — O'Neal — what is going on here?"

"Well, sir, you caught us!" blurted Bruno. "The Phantom was us all along!"

"We lied!" babbled Boots. "We're liars! There isn't an honest bone in our bodies!"

"You're probably going to have to expel us again," Bruno added. "And this time make it stick."

The Headmaster stared at them in amazement. Finally,

he said, "You will return to your beds at once."

"Oh, that's not a good idea, sir," said Bruno confidentially. "We're dangerous. Look what we did. We wrote *Goodyear* on that poster, after all of Chris's hard work."

Mr. Sturgeon intensified his steely grey stare. "The only crime of which you boys are guilty is rewriting the curfew rules of Macdonald Hall. Don't you two ever sleep? Get to bed this instant!"

Very reluctantly, Bruno and Boots slunk out of the Faculty Building.

The Headmaster waited until the heavy doors shut behind them. He cleared his throat. "Mildred, you can come out now."

His wife flipped open the lid of the lost-and-found box, and stepped out. "Oh, hello, William. Working late, are we?"

He turned to her. "Tell me, Mildred. Tell me extraterrestrials kidnapped you and replaced you with one of their own. It was this creature, not you, who was the Phantom. Please tell me that, Mildred. Because from where I stand, it seems as though my wife of forty years has gone stark-raving mad!"

"Oh, William," she exclaimed. "I did it for you!"

He gawked. "For *me?* Why couldn't you just knit me a nice pair of socks? How could you possibly think that reducing this school to utter chaos was something you should do for *me?*"

She put her hands on her hips and regarded him sternly. "At the beginning of this year you were turning into an old fuddy-duddy! You transformed a simple ingrown toenail into a heart transplant! Every second word out of your mouth was *retirement* because your job had no challenge for you anymore. So I *gave* you a challenge. I created a whole big mystery so you could see just how much this school needs you. Heaven knows you need this school!"

The Headmaster was struck dumb. He looked at his wife for a long time. Finally, he spoke. "Unbelievable as it may seem, I think I understand."

"You're welcome," she said crisply.

"I suppose I *have* been a little difficult to live with," he went on grudgingly.

"Like a bear with a sore nose," his wife confirmed.

"You may be certain that we're going to be at Macdonald Hall for a long time. And first thing tomorrow morning, I shall telephone Dr. Haupt and schedule the operation on my toe."

She threw her arms around him. "Oh, William!"

Chapter 20

earsplitting, teeth-rattling ...

Under the laser web on Miss Scrimmage's front property crawled Elmer and Edward. Both boys were soaked to the skin. The sprinklers had wet down the lawn, and there was mud everywhere. Covered in slime, they inhaled dead leaves and exhaled clumps of grass.

"How much further?" gurgled Edward miserably.

Elmer looked up, but all he could see was the mist of the sprinklers and the criss-crossing red lasers. He dared not raise his head above the spray for fear of breaking one of the beams, and setting off the alarm. "We're close! Extremely close!" he lied. Inside, he thought, *We'll never make it. We'll trip the alarm and be caught and expelled.* He might never get his chance with Marylou.

He forced the spray, the mud and the danger to the back of his mind. His muscles were screaming with exhaustion. Behind him he could make out Edward — a squirming mass of muck.

Bump! His head came up against something hard. He rolled over onto his back and opened his eyes. He was at the foot of the wrought-iron fence! Outside the laser web! He was free!

He grabbed Edward and pulled him up to the fence. "We made it!" he exulted, ripping off his muddy stocking cap and throwing it high in the air. A gust of chill November wind caught the hat and blew it back toward the school.

Elmer and Edward watched in helpless agony as the knit cap descended into the laser web, cutting its way through the beams like a hot knife through butter.

The SectorWatch Fortress Ultra-Deluxe Banshee II alarm detonated the night in a supernova of pure noise. Sixty-seven loudspeakers roared to life, blaring a combination of sirens, horns, bells, buzzers and Klaxons. Every window at Miss Scrimmage's school instantly shattered, the glass shooting six metres from the building. Red emergency beacons flashed all over, and the giant searchlight on the roof began sweeping the yard.

Elmer and Edward stood at the foot of the fence, bellowing at each other. But even a shriek directly into an ear could not be heard over the Banshee II. Girls in pink nighties began to appear in what was left of their windows, hands over their ears, faces contorted. At Macdonald Hall, pyjama-clad boys streamed out of the dormitories to investigate the disturbance. Even there, three football fields away, the noise of the alarm was unbearable.

Bruno and Boots were halfway back to their room when the alarm went off. In the crowd of boys pouring out onto the campus, Bruno pounced on the first familiar face. It was Pete Anderson.

"What's going on?" he bellowed.

"Yeah, it's pretty loud!" replied Pete.

Larry Wilson ran up to them, shivering in shorts and a T-shirt. *"It's Scrimmage's alarm!"* he shouted. *"And I hate to tell you, Boots — I just checked. Your brother's missing!"*

Boots looked at Bruno. *"What are we going to do?"*

"Let him rot?" suggested Bruno hopefully. But even as he said it, he knew they had to rescue Edward. *"Let's go!"*

* * *

Cathy Burton barrelled into her room, still carrying the salami she had been slicing. Desperately, she yanked apart the wire Elmer had reconnected, but this had no effect. She screamed urgently at Diane, who screamed urgently back. Neither could make out a single word. Inside Scrimmage's, the Banshee II was an earsplitting, teeth-rattling, gut-shaking, brain-melting roar. It was almost like the total silence of outer space, because the horrible din blocked out all other sound.

Completely unable to communicate, Cathy threw open a drawer, and began digging through a pile of underwear, firing it in all directions. At last, she emerged with the "borrowed" SectorWatch Instruction Manual.

Diane understood at once. There had to be some way to turn off the Banshee II before it busted every eardrum at Scrimmage's.

Shoulder to shoulder, the girls windmilled through the manual, frantically searching for something that would

shut down the alarm — C for Cancel, D
for Off, Q for Quiet — *anything!*

That was when Diane saw it:

OUTER ELECTRIFIED WIRE
In an alarm situation, the perimeter wire becon   .
fied to prevent intruders from escaping from the p emises.

The two exchanged a horrified look. Elmer and Edward
didn't know about that wire! They were going to be *fried!*

They ran out of their room. The halls were bedlam.
Students were bumping into each other, scrambling in all
directions, as though trying to outrun the paralyzing
noise. Girls tied towels around their heads, and stuffed
cotton in their ears. Two were in a tug-of-war over a pair
of airline ear protectors. Rex cowered under a table; he
seemed to be barking wildly, although no one could hear
it.

Through all this chaos charged Miss Scrimmage,
shrieking instructions and loading fresh shells into her
shotgun. The alarm was the last thing on her mind. An
intruder was loose on the campus and she was going to
defend her students.

Cathy and Diane raced down the main stairs and
burst out the front door. They paused in surprise at
finding the sprinklers on and the laser web illuminated
like a red neon connect-the-dots. Then the searchlight
fell on the wrought-iron fence. For a moment, there they
were, Elmer and Edward, halfway up, captured in the
beam like flies in amber. Along the top of the fence the
girls could make out the electrified wire — innocent-

w, but when somebody touched it —
.wo girls ran out into the spray and mud.

* * *

Bruno and Boots lost the ability to talk to each other at the edge of the highway. The alarm was too loud and too close.

Communicating by hand signals and lip reading, they raced across the road.

Suddenly, Boots pointed. About twenty metres down, near the front gate, there was Edward and another boy. Bruno and Boots stared at each other and mouthed the word in unison: *"Elmer?"*

It was hard to be sure. Both fugitives were filthy from head to toe. The added weight of all that mud and their heavy wet clothes, plus near-total exhaustion, were making the climb slow and awkward.

Out of the laser-riddled sprinkler mist appeared Cathy and Diane, neck and neck in a full sprint, screaming and pointing at the top of the fence.

Bruno and Boots looked at each other and shrugged.

And then some mist from a sprinkler head drifted over the wrought-iron gate. A small shower of sparks shot out of the electrified wire.

"Edward!" screamed Boots at the top of his lungs. *"The wire! Stay away from the wire!"* Nobody heard him over the Banshee II. He didn't even hear himself.

The two climbers were nearing the electrified wire. If they touched it soaking wet like they were — Edward heaved himself up to reach for the top.

"No-o-o-o!!" chorused Bruno, Boots, Cathy and Diane. Their warning was swallowed by the roar of the alarm.

Edward's muddy hand began to close on the top of the fence and the electrified wire.

The door to Miss Scrimmage's second-floor balcony was kicked open. Out stomped the Headmistress, curlers awry, eyes wild, shotgun levelled. She tripped over a little watering can, kicking it off her balcony. As she struggled to maintain her balance, she accidentally fired both barrels of the shotgun. The gun's recoil knocked Miss Scrimmage back inside the balcony doors.

The shells ripped into a power-line transformer just as Edward's hand clamped down on the top wire. Hundreds of faces turned upward to watch the fireworks display as the transformer exploded, spewing fountains of sparks and colour. Electricity was knocked out for everything within ten kilometres of the exploded power line — including the SectorWatch top wire. Edward and then Elmer clambered over the fence and jumped to the ground.

The dying transformer sizzled out. Both campuses went dark. And silent.

* * *

Boots held the flashlight while his brother Edward showered off the many layers of mud he had picked up on Miss Scrimmage's front lawn. The younger boy's clothes were already in the garbage Dumpster behind the dormitories.

Edward shampooed his hair for the fourth time. "I'll bet a lot of guys are going to be late for class tomorrow — no lights, no clocks. And what's going to be for breakfast? Cold cereal? Sour milk? Untoasted toast? Raw eggs?"

"Cut the comedy and hurry up," growled Boots. "Boy, I

"always knew you were a pain. But until tonight, I didn't realize you were nuts."

"Mom must be here. I hear Mom," said Edward innocently. He sniffed. "Hey, what do they use for fertilizer at Scrimmage's? I still stink."

"I mean, if you needed help with math, why didn't you come to me?" said Boots as though no one had spoken. "Or Bruno? Better still, Elmer. He *invented* math! But no. You had to do it the hard way. You had to crawl under a laser web and risk putting eight million volts through your stupid carcass! I can just picture myself calling up Mom with the big news that her little darling is a charcoal briquette!"

"Aha!" Edward turned off the water and wrapped himself in a towel. "You were worried."

Boots took a step back. "Was not," he said defensively.

"Were, too."

"Maybe a little," Boots admitted grudgingly. "Even though you're a moron, you're still my brother."

Edward sniffled. "That was beautiful!" he wept emotionally.

Boots was unmoved. Edward could turn on fake tears at the drop of a hat. He switched off the flashlight, leaving them in the dark.

"Hey, turn that back on," said Edward, back to his old self.

"Not until you promise to behave," said Boots. "And I want to hear you say that we old men aren't ready for the scrap heap yet."

"Hey," came Edward's reply. "You 'old men' sure came through for me tonight!"

Boots turned on the light again. "I'm gla
started to appreciate Bruno. I always told you
amazing — "

"Bruno?" Edward interrupted with a snort. "He's the
same jerk he always was. But that guy Drimsdale — man,
is he cool under fire! He lives on the *edge!*"

Chapter 21

simple surgery

Mr. Sturgeon was true to his word. Three days after SectorWatch Inc. removed the Fortress Ultra-Deluxe from Miss Scrimmage's Finishing School for Young Ladies, he checked into Toronto General Hospital for the operation on his ingrown toenail.

It was a simple procedure. He would spend the night at the hospital, undergo surgery at eight the next morning, and be home by late afternoon.

In his private room, the Headmaster did a little reading, telephoned his wife to say goodnight, and switched off his bedside light. He was almost asleep — in that dreamlike state between waking and slumber — when a strange feeling came over him. And he knew with absolute certainty that he was being watched.

Disturbed, he opened his eyes and saw, in some alarm, that there were two dark figures standing by the side of his bed.

"Good heavens!" He sat bolt upright and switched on the light. There stood Bruno Walton and Boots O'Neal. "Have you both lost your minds?" the Headmaster raged. "How on *earth* did you get here?"

"A taxi," Bruno admitted. "That got us to the commuter train. We took the subway once we hit town."

"We had a little trouble figuring out the subway map," Boots added. "Sorry to be bothering you so late. How do you feel, sir?"

"I am furious, of course!" Mr. Sturgeon exploded. "How should I feel when I run into two of my students, after lights-out, 70 kilometres from school?"

"Not *that* kind of feel, sir," Bruno corrected. "How do you feel medically?"

The Headmaster ignored the question. "This goes beyond anything, even for you two! How dare you defy my rules to such an appalling degree? And then dance around in my face like you're proud of it?"

"Shhh!" cautioned Bruno. "Sir, this is a hospital."

"Explain yourselves!" bellowed the patient.

The boys exchanged a meaningful look. When Bruno spoke again there were tears in his eyes. "Sir, we talked it over and we decided that we don't care if we get in trouble, or wash dishes, or even get expelled. You've been our Headmaster for a long time and we couldn't pass up the chance to see you one last time."

"One last time?" Mr. Sturgeon repeated, bewildered.

"Well," Bruno explained gently, "the operation is tomorrow so we wanted to see you tonight just in case you don't make it."

The Headmaster frowned. "Don't make what?"

"You know," Bruno persisted. "What if you — like — well — uh — *die?*"

Mr. Sturgeon's eyes bulged. "Die?"

Both boys nodded sombrely.

"But it's only an ingrown toenail!"

Bruno and Boots stared in shock.

"It *is?*" gasped Boots. "You mean, like, a sore foot?"

The Headmaster was genuinely touched. "What in the world gave you the idea that I was at death's door?"

Bruno shrugged. "Well, the cane and the limp. And then we started hearing stuff about hospitals and operations and how nothing else was going to do any good — so we put two and two together."

"And came up with five," concluded the patient. "Boys, this is a very simple surgery. I'll be back at my desk by the end of the week." He added, "You seem disappointed, Walton."

"Oh, no, sir," said Bruno. "It's great news that you're okay. It's just that — well, we're going to wash a lot of dishes for this and an ingrown toenail sort of isn't worth it."

"I'm sorry," Mr. Sturgeon said sarcastically. "How inconsiderate of me. Perhaps I should ask the doctors for a new spleen. Would that do?"

Boots studied the floor. "We're really going to get creamed over this one, aren't we, sir?"

The Headmaster was disposed to be kind. "I suppose

your hearts were in the right place." He sighed. "And at least you didn't involve anybody else in this lunatic enterprise."

"Right," agreed Bruno. "I mean, sort of . . . uh, not too many."

The Headmaster sat forward in alarm. "Do you mean to tell me that there are Macdonald Hall students roaming around this hospital?"

"Oh, no, sir," Boots blurted. "They're all waiting downstairs in the lobby. We're the only ones who could outrun the security guard."

"If you see anybody, sir," Bruno requested, "could you kind of pretend to be sicker than you really are? Because we all went through a lot of trouble to get here and the others are going to be pretty steamed if they find out you're not dying."

"I most certainly will not!" Mr. Sturgeon exclaimed angrily. "This is not a television sitcom — "

The door flew open and in bounded four young doctors in green surgical scrubs. The four ripped away their masks and stood before their Headmaster — Pete Anderson, Larry Wilson, Mark Davies and Wilbur Hackenschleimer.

"Sir, how are you?" asked Pete anxiously.

"I'm feeling *very tired*," said Mr. Sturgeon through clenched teeth.

"How do you stop this thing?" cried a familiar voice. Sidney Rampulsky sped into the room, riding an out-of-control wheelchair. He executed a spectacular wheelie and bailed out a split second before the chair smashed into the wall.

Sidney sat up, rubbing his head. "Is there a doctor in the house?"

Pete nudged Larry. "Boy, Mr. Sturgeon really is sick," he whispered. "His face is turning purple."

Next came Edward O'Neal, pushing a long medical gurney. The sheet on top stirred, and out peered Cathy Burton and Diane Grant.

"Hello, sir!" called Cathy. "We came to wish you luck!"

Mr. Sturgeon looked daggers at Bruno and Boots. "You neglected to mention that a few of the young ladies came along for the ride." His bedside phone began to ring. "Ah, that must be Miss Scrimmage now. No doubt she's just noticed that some of her students are missing."

"Don't answer it, sir," Diane pleaded.

"Believe me, Miss Grant, I do not wish to deal with your Headmistress tonight any more than you do."

The ringing stopped.

Elmer Drimsdale and Marylou Beakman brought up the rear. "I used to stand on the lawn," Elmer was saying, "trying to work up the courage to go over and talk to you. One night the crest on my T-shirt was recorded on video and I became a suspect. They thought I was the Phantom."

"But who was the *real* Phantom?" asked Marylou.

"Nobody knows," Mark supplied. "But when I printed my special *Student Times* on the big riot, the headline had been tampered with. I ended up running off three hundred copies of *PHANTOM RETIRES — SO LONG, SUCKERS.*" He shook his head. "I still can't figure out how he got to the press. Mrs. Sturgeon was watching the print shop the whole time!"

Elmer nodded. "The Phantom was remarkably clever. Maybe *he'd* know how to get me out of the Music-by-Mail Record Club."

Mark Davies held a mini tape recorder under Mr. Sturgeon's nose. "Sir, do you have any final comments for the *Student Times?*"

"I've had enough!" bellowed the Headmaster, standing up on his bed. "It is time for this madness to stop! I am a very sick man, facing delicate surgery! I do not have the strength to participate in a circus!"

A shocked silence fell. Mr. Sturgeon looked at the cowed faces and noted with satisfaction that he had control of the room.

"Out! Out! All of you! You will all go to the waiting room, where you will *wait!* I shall call Mr. Flynn and he will be making arrangements to pick you up. *Dismissed!*"

Obediently, the chastened students began to file out of the room.

Bruno and Boots were the last to leave.

Bruno paused at the door. "Thanks, sir, for not telling them about the ingrown toenail."

"What made you change your mind?" added Boots.

The Headmaster resettled himself on his bed. "You boys are fully aware that my wife was the notorious Phantom. And yet no one else knows and none of the usual rumours have been circulating. Boys, I am very grateful that, out of respect for me, you have decided to keep silent."

Boots looked surprised. "It had nothing to do with respect, sir."

Mr. Sturgeon was taken aback. "Then why didn't you tell?"

"Well, we wanted to," explained Bruno. "We were just about to spread it around to all the guys. But then it hit us — who would believe it? That sounds like the stupidest joke of all!"

about the author

It has been twenty-five years since the publication of Gordon Korman's first Macdonald Hall novel, written when he was only twelve. He went on to write five more books before he even finished high school.

He now has more than fifty books to his credit, including six more Macdonald Hall titles, and, most recently, *Son of the Mob*, *Jake, Reinvented* and the *Dive* trilogy. He lives with his family in Long Island, New York, where he looks forward to his second quarter-century of writing for kids.

Be sure to check out these other hilarious Macdonald Hall adventures!

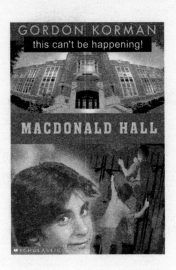

This Can't be Happening!

Bruno Walton and Boots O'Neal are in their second year at Macdonald Hall, a fine boarding school for boys. They're best friends — and roommates. That is, until Headmaster Sturgeon decides to separate them.

Boots finds himself bunking with George Wexford-Smyth III, a rich hypochondriac, while Bruno gets stuck with science-geek Elmer Drimsdale. But they won't let that spoil their school year. Oh no. Whatever it takes, Bruno and Boots will be reunited. Even skunk stunts and an ant stampede can't keep them apart.

And that's only the beginning.

The first fearlessly funny book in the Macdonald Hall series.

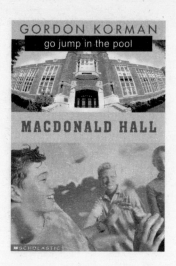

Go Jump in the Pool

For the students of Macdonald Hall, there's nothing worse than losing to York Academy, but until the Hall gets its own pool, those York turkeys will win every swim meet.

But the Hall is fifty thousand dollars short of getting their own pool. School pride is plummeting. There's even talk of Boots's father transferring him to York Academy. So it's Bruno Walton to the rescue. He's the man with the plan. How hard can it be to raise fifty grand? A few bake sales, a talent show, a rummage sale . . . they'll come up with the cash in no time, won't they?

Won't they?

The second fearlessly funny book in the Macdonald Hall series.

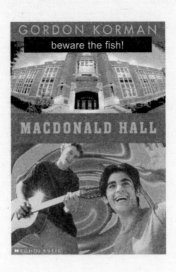

Beware the Fish

Macdonald Hall is having a serious cash-flow problem. Everything is being cut back — evening snack is gone, the lab equipment is decrepit and the dorms are freezing. Worst of all, Mr. Sturgeon is closing Dormitory 3, forcing Bruno and Boots to bunk with Elmer Drimsdale.

Is this the end of Canada's finest boarding school?

Puh-leese. This is Bruno and Boots we're talking about — they always have a plan. If they can just get some major publicity, score some big media attention, then tons of new students will enroll and the dough will start pouring in. There's just one problem: the cops are closing in on them . . .

The third fearlessly funny book in the Macdonald Hall series.

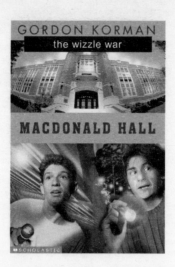

The Wizzle War

Macdonald Hall is under attack. Where once tradition and freedom of speech ruled the campus, now there is Mr. Wizzle.

That means a dress code — ties, even. Demerit points for just breathing the wrong way. Psychological tests for all students. Surprise dorm inspections. All in the name of progress. But the students won't stand for it. Wizzle doesn't stand a chance against The Committee — a secret society of Macdonald Hall loyalists who meet late at night to plot their revenge.

Whether it takes toilet-paper rolls, a touch of romance or even an earthquake, it's unanimous: Wizzle must go!

The fourth fearlessly funny book in the Macdonald Hall series.

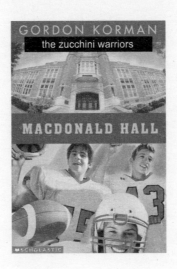

The Zucchini Warriors

Bruno and Boots worked hard on their petition for a new recreation centre. So when they return to school in the fall and find a football stadium instead, they're less than excited. Macdonald Hall doesn't even have a football team!

Their benefactor Hank the Tank Carson offers the students a deal. If they can put together a winning team, he'll build them their rec centre. The only problem is, the Macdonald Warriors stink.

Fortunately for them, there's a star quarterback in their midst. Or at least close by. And the fact that she attends Miss Scrimmage's Finishing School for Young Ladies . . . well, that'll just make this season even more interesting!

The fifth fearlessly funny book in the Macdonald Hall series.

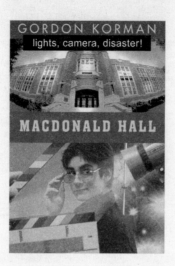

Lights, Camera, Disaster!

It's fabulous. It's perfect. Macdonald Hall has been chosen as the set for a Hollywood movie, staring Jordie Jones. This is just the breakthrough Bruno has been waiting for. He'll do anything to be in the movie, and Boots will do anything to keep him out of trouble. And the girls at Miss Scrimmage's? They'll do anything to meet Jordie Jones.

Bruno and Boots soon discover that the star just wants to be a normal guy, one who plays hockey, hangs out with friends and goes to dances. So they decide to help Jordie out. What could possibly go wrong? Except anything and everything . . .

The sixth fearlessly funny book in the Macdonald Hall series.